SHADES

OF

LOVE

HEDGEHOG HILL PRESS

An imprint of

NJZ Enterprises
7 Urban Drive
Anderson, Indiana 46011

A Hedgehog Hill Press original, 2016

ISBN: 978-0692785171

DEDICATION

I dedicate this to all of those men in my life who have added the spark, the beauty, and yes, the shades of love, to get me to the place I am today. You have loved me in different ways at different times and for different reasons, but you have added to the tapestry of my life in ways that I will never be able to express. Thank you, my loves.

ACKNOWLEDGEMENT

I would like to thank the following people for their input about this story. Their comments have proven invaluable:

First thanks go to my wonderful editor, Heather Harrold. Without her, the book would be filled with errors. She offered advice and expertise when needed. Thanks Heather.

Next, my thanks go to Rebekah Raffield. She read the story and came up with the perfect cover that expresses the feeling that I hoped the story achieved.

Great thanks to my beta readers: Helen Davies, JB Brines, and Sandra Kolb. Your suggestions were incorporated when possible and were appreciated more than I can express.

Thanks to those men and women who braved the sixties and helped mold our world. To those veterans of Vietnam, we thank you for your service. We also thank those individuals who were able to look beyond the color of a person's skin to find love and happiness during a difficult decade in our history. Bless you all.

Disclaimer

This story is a work of fiction. There are places and figures who actually exist or existed during the sixties. The characters of the story are not modeled after any person living or dead. Events and locations that actually existed have been used in order to create this work of fiction and should not be considered to be historically accurate.

SHADES
OF
LOVE

BY
Nancy Zimmerman

Meeting Sylvia

U.S. Naval Academy

Standing at the entrance of the U.S. Naval Academy at Annapolis, Maryland, Ron Michaels just shook his head. His parents were very proud of the young man he had become. It was not every young black man who could get an appointment to Annapolis. He and his parents had Senator Stephen M. Young to thank for the honor, and Ron was determined to do his family, his state, and his nation proud.

He lifted his suitcase and walked into the compound which would be his home for the next four years. He was looking forward to the experiences that he would have in the service. As he walked toward Bancroft Hall he had time to consider how different his life would be from here on in. Both sets of his grandparents were in Virginia and as they were aging, his parents felt that it would be a good time for them to move to the east coast. His dad, James, had left the family restaurant business years earlier when his mother, Amelia, had found a teaching job in Dayton, Ohio. James had taken his restaurant experience with him and had two successful restaurants in Dayton for many years. With Ron, their only child, leaving home, the move east would also keep them closer to him for at least the next few years.

Ron had an easy manner about him, but during the more intense training, all who knew him grew to appreciate that quality as he quickly defeated most of them in contests of strength and endurance. He had not only a quick wit but also a compassionate and his superiors saw his leadership potential very quickly.

The autumn of 1960 brought about the first televised presidential debate on September 26th between Vice President Richard M. Nixon and Senator John Kennedy. It was an interesting series of debates as the two men met four separate times to discuss the various issues facing the country. Ron, whose parents were lifelong Democrats, was impressed by the young senator from Massachusetts. He continued to follow the debates right through the election where John Kennedy became the thirty-fifth president of the United States.

As Kennedy was sworn in on January 20, 1961, Ron was standing in the crowd as the the new President's words came across the speakers and burrowed their way into his being: "Ask not what your country can do for you, ask what you can do for your country. Ask not what America can do for you but what together we can do for the freedom of man." Ron did not realize how these words would help him as he furthered his training in the Marines.

Goodbye Plebe, Hello Cadet Michaels

"Hey, Ron, we're headed over to Dahlgren Hall, you coming with us?"

Ron looked up from his textbook and brushed a hand over his head as he shook it from side to side. "Nope, not tonight, I have too much to do to get ready for this project. Thanks for the invite, though. Maybe next time."

"Sure thing buddy, see ya."

Ron got up and popped the tab to a soft drink, taking a big swallow as he looked out the window. He had been at Annapolis for over a year now. This last year, on August 21st, the Department of the Interior designated the Academy as a National Historical Landmark. Because of his naval career, President Kennedy had been there for the ceremony, and Ron had the opportunity to shake his hand and thank him both for his service and for providing such an example as a role model. It was a moment Ron would always remember.

Ron turned back to his desk and his studies. He was thinking about participating in an experimental program that would become fully integrated in 1963 as the Trident Scholar Program.

His second school year was quickly coming to an end. Ron had become accustomed to life at the

Academy and while some of the cadets moaned over the regulations and lack of freedom, Ron did not see it that way. The students could get passes to get into town, and occasionally anyone could sign up for some of the tours to nearby historical sites. Ron found himself enjoying the opportunities to see this part of the country and its rich history. He also enjoyed calling on a particular girl in town when he knew he had an evening off campus. At 6'2" tall and 210 pounds, he was a good-looking young man with dark chocolate colored skin and coal black eyes.

While some women's eyes automatically followed him as their heads turned when he walked by, Ron tried not to notice because he lived his life carefully. In some respects, he did not care how he was viewed by others. This was a time, however, when it also served a black man well to be aware of his surroundings but not to appear to look in any one direction too long. The times were getting more and more tense for the Negro population.

Because Ron grew up in Dayton, Ohio, his friends were an assembly of cultures and so he did not have the same outlook about race that most of his contemporaries, both Negro and Caucasian, shared. He had learned that while there was a tolerance for crossing the racial lines in the Academy, it often didn't transfer to the town itself. The men of the town guarded their young women carefully, regardless of their race or age. Those young cadets in their uniforms looked mighty tempting to the young women of Annapolis and more than one fight had started when a cadet had approached a girl who was already "taken." Ron himself had been on the other side of a fist when one girl's brother or cousin had come to defend her honor against the "black nigger son of a bitch." If for no other reason than these dangers, Ron and a few of his buddies waited until they got to Washington, DC to fraternize with the females.

As Ron sat back down at his desk, he looked over his summer schedule. He could be participating in one of the honors programs but was opting to get into the Service Academy Exchange Program, or SAEP, and work with the USMC for a while. As his junior year ended and arrangements were made for the exchange program, Ron was partnered with Brad Carver, a freshman, and the two young men found that they shared an appreciation for the discipline that the military afforded as well as an appreciation for a curvaceous feminine figure. They were both looking forward to a little bit of freedom in relation to their personal schedules. Despite the age difference, they got along very well and their friendship developed into one that was a good fit for them both.

The time they shared in DC was not as easy as they had hoped. Race relations in the summer of 1963 were heating up. Birmingham, Alabama had been home to protests where dogs and fire hoses were turned on the protestors, and, while that was one of the most public protests, there were others all over the country. Reverend Martin Luther King, Jr. had become a leader in the civil rights fight and was planning a march to DC for the fall. President Kennedy had presented civil rights legislation, but it was being stalled in Congress. People on both sides became more fired up as the tension built. The President had been a bit leery of the march, thinking that it would cause some of the members of Congress to withhold approval of the proposed legislation, but as plans continued, he put his support behind it.

One Fine Day

It was during the late summer that Brad had a visitor from home. His neighbor, Sylvia Greene, and her friend Jenny Lester were in the capital city enjoying the last few weeks of their summer vacation before they went back to school at IU after Labor Day. Sylvia and Brad laughed, joked, and had a relationship that seemed more to Ron like siblings than anything else but he still found himself a little envious. Sylvia had clearly brought Jenny to DC to introduce him to Brad. She was Brad's kind of girl. Curvy and sassy. She could take as good as she could give and the two were off and running as they began talking. Sylvia was quiet but her eyes sparkled as she looked up at Ron and grinned.

"I knew Brad would take to her."

"Oh, yeah?" said Ron. "Now how were you so sure...? You gals made an awfully long trip on that assumptlon."

"I have known Brad Carver as long as I can remember. I know the kind of girl he goes for. He and I actually went out on a date once or twice. I love him to pieces but when it came to kissing him good night, it just seemed strange. He is like a brother to me. I also know Jenny, and she is goodness in the body of a stripper." Sylvia blushed when she said this and looked away. Turning back, she said, "I usually don't talk like that, but somehow I knew you would understand how I meant it."

Ron knew at that moment he had found a woman he wanted to get to know much better. There was a problem, however, a big problem. Sylvia was white. Sylvia was a Midwestern white girl who had been brought up in a conservative fashion. He was reasonably certain that dating a Negro was not something that would be approved of within her family's parameters of acceptability, but he knew that he had to get to know her better. Hopefully they could establish a friendship that would survive their distance through letters and occasional phone calls and see where it would take them. He had cousins who were in biracial relationships, and he knew from them how difficult it was to establish and nurture those with the current situations in the country. He decided she was worth the effort and smiled back at her, winking as he said it, "I think I know exactly what you mean. It will be funny to watch Brad meet his match."

The foursome spent as much time as they could together considering the hours that the men were working. Because they were attached to the military, Brad and Ron had options for tours and access to places that most of the tourists never go to see. They both felt that it was up to them as hosts to provide the best experiences they could for the ladies for the two weeks they were going to be there.

It was a typical hot summer and this August was proving to be one of the hottest of recent years. The Civil Rights march was planned for the next week, about three days before the girls were expecting to go home. Ron felt that he was causing the group a lot of problems as they were not admitted to a couple of restaurants. They assured him that he wasn't, but he opted to stay home from an outdoor concert they had planned on attending.

Sylvia was beginning to feel like she was in love. She wasn't sure when it happened. Perhaps it had been when he extended felt his hand to shake hers when they were introduced and she felt a tingling all the way up her arm. Perhaps it was when he winked at her when they discussed Brad and Jenny. Or, maybe it was when he quietly reached down at the Botanical Gardens and picked up a small stone with a very definite heart shape and gave it to her as he said, "Here is a heart, from me to you. I hope you will always remember this time favorably."

She was not about to go to a concert without Ron. There were so few days left. She and Ron had been on their own a few times as Brad and Jenny wandered off to spend some time alone. "Well, I have a great idea. Why don't we stop by the grocery, pick up some food, and you and I can go back to your place and fix pizza while we give Brad and Jenny some time to enjoy the concert together. Really, a slow evening with a chance to take off my shoes and relax sounds great. We can always put records on if we want to dance."

Brad and Jenny thought it sounded like a good plan so they went their separate ways. It was about four in the afternoon and they had stopped to get the makings for a fantastic supper when a couple of guys stepped out in front of Ron.

"Hey there, nigger! Whatcha doin with this fine white girl?"

"Excuse us, please, we are on our way to meet friends," Ron replied as respectfully as he could. He wanted to get Sylvia away from this situation as quickly as possible. He smelled beer on the guy's breath and sensed they were ready for a fight. He handed the bag of groceries to Sylvia along with the key to the apartment and told her he would be there in a few moments. Sylvia hesitated but Ron lifted his chin in a way that told her, "go on, I will be fine," so she left. "Now, gentlemen, what is it you want me to know?"

The two looked at each other. They were not used to having to stand and be confronted. They worked as a pair so they could intimidate any of the Negroes they came across. It had always worked and afterwards it gave them a lot to brag about to their buddies. "You just need to get your raggedy black ass off the street... It's gonna be gettin dark soon and you need to be home."

"Well, if I have it figured right, I probably have about four hours and forty-three minutes -- give or take a couple of minutes -- before that becomes a problem. So, now that we have that problem solved, what else do we need to work on?" Ron knew he was playing a dangerous game but the drinks the guys had were catching up with them, and he knew if he did not find a way to tone down the situation, there would be bloodshed.

The two men became more confused as they contemplated Ron. They looked around and saw a white cop and called to him, "Hey there, you, Cop!"

The policeman turned and gave a slight shudder. He had dealt with these two guys before, and he knew what they liked to do to intimidate anyone they could, Negroes, women, old folks. They were just bullies, plain and simple, but one of the guys was the son of a Congressman from Alabama so he had clout. "What can I do for you Chip?"

"Hey, you know me? Yeah, I remember seeing you before. I want you to arrest this guy. He was bothering me and my buddy here. We were just minding our own business, and he stopped us looking for a fight."

"Hmmm, is that so? Well, why don't you guys get along and I will talk to him and see what is going on."

"Nah, I think we will watch and make sure he doesn't give you any problems when you arrest him."

"Can I have your name, sir?" the policeman asked Ron.

"Ron Michaels, Midshipman 1st Class, at the Naval Academy. I'm here in DC on an exchange program with the Marine Corps, sir. I will be happy to share my contact information down at the station."

The policeman breathed a sigh of relief. The Midshipman had just made it possible for him to diffuse the situation and keep everyone satisfied. He gave a nod to Ron then said, "If you will come with me, I am taking you to the station."

The two bullies heckled Ron until he was in the back seat of the cruiser then started laughing and went on their way.

"My name is Bobby, Bobby Wilson," he said as he reached around to extend his hand to Ron. "Thanks for your quick thinking out there. Those guys are a pain in the ass. That short cock sucker has a daddy in Congress and he thinks his shit doesn't stink. And the fact is, in this town, it doesn't. Daddy is chairman of a couple of important committees and makes sure that he keeps the kid out of trouble using his influence. I have had a couple of run ins myself and it isn't pleasant."

"I understand, sir. Now, if we can just get this taken care of quickly, I have friends to meet."

"Where can I drop you? I am not taking you in," Bobby laughed, started the car, and began driving to the address Ron had given him.

Ron went up the steps and opened the door to the apartment, shouting to Sylvia, "It's me."

She ran in from the kitchen and threw her arms around his neck and held on as he wrapped his arms around her waist and held her. "I told you I would be back."

"I know, but I was so worried. Those guys were awful... I should have stayed there. I am sorry I was such a chicken."

At that, Ron reached up and took her hands from around his neck and held them. "You are no chicken. Don't ever think that. You are a beautiful kind woman who simply cannot understand the cruelty and hate that lives in other people."

Sylvia had tears streaming down her cheeks as she looked into his eyes. "I am falling in love with you, Ron."

"Well," he said as he pulled her back into his embrace, "Since I love you, that is very nice to hear. Now, let's get to working on the pizza while we talk about this." He released her with a kiss to the temple.

The two put on some music they both enjoyed and went to the kitchen to chop the onions, peppers, and mushrooms for the pizza. Jenny and Brad came through the doors about 8 pm and stopped as they saw Ron and Sylvia in an embrace as they slowly danced to Ruby and the Romantics singing, "Our Day Will Come." The two looked at each other and winked. Jenny and Brad had seen this coming and Brad couldn't be happier for them both. They were two of the best people he had ever had in his life. He put his arm around Jenny's waist and pulled her closer. This was a fine young lady, too, but he knew she was not his forever, just a wonderful new friend. Jenny felt the same way. She knew that Sylvia had hoped she and Brad would hit it off romantically, and there was an attraction, just not that "until death do you part" kind of love attraction. They smiled then joined Ron and Sylvia as they danced.

The girls were scheduled to go home in two days but they were going to be there for the March on Washington. They all decided that it would be a historical event worth attending.

Earlier in the year, May, to be exact, there were televised scenes of children being knocked off their feet by water powerful enough it was said to rip the bark off of trees. After this was televised, the polls showed a jump from 4% to 52% of people who agreed that civil rights was the country's most pressing issue. In the months that followed there were over seven hundred marches in over one hundred fifty cities resulting in over fourteen thousand arrests. It was during this time that the march on Washington was organized by Bayard Rustin.

The citizens of the United States had experienced a year of turmoil. George Wallace had stood in a schoolhouse door to block the entrance of the University of Alabama in an attempt to keep three black students from attending. Later that evening, President Kennedy had addressed the nation denouncing segregation and informing the country of his intent to submit a comprehensive civil rights bill to Congress. Within twenty-four hours, a leader of the NAACP, Medgar Evers, was killed in the driveway of his home. These events stoked the fires that were lighting up the streets in the United States that year.

This march was intended to be a stance for jobs and freedom. Most of white America was neither supportive nor did they think it would make a difference. Nevertheless, at a time when marches on Washington were rare, about a quarter of a million people showed up, about 25% white, to support the Negro community and their fight for equal rights.

The four friends were a part of that march and as they heard the stirring words of the Reverend Martin Luther King, Jr., Sylvia reached over and took Ron's hand in hers and gave it a squeeze. He looked down as she looked up at him with tears in her beautiful blue eyes. "Maybe someday," she said.

Sylvia Ponders Life

"You cannot be serious!" Jenny exclaimed, eyes wide open gaping at her friend.

"I am dead serious," Sylvia replied. "I intend to marry Ron. Someday, someway, we will be together."

"Oh, dear Lord. You just met the guy. Give me a break," Jenny replied as she continued painting her toenails a bright red. "Your mom and dad will have fits! NO, I take that back. They will just drop dead from the shock."

Sylvia bit her lip. She had been back only a few days, but she missed Ron. She knew that if her parents only met Ron, they would understand. She could have Brad pave the way. He could introduce him as his friend and they could all hang out together. It would work, it just had to. "I think you misunderstand what I am thinking," she replied to Jenny. "I have to get through school first. Ron and Brad are going to be in the service for a few years. There will be opportunities for mom and dad to meet Ron without knowing how much he means to me."

"A few years! Sylvia, listen to yourself. Ron and Brad are in for twenty years at the least. They are making a career out of it, at least Ron is. He is at Annapolis. That isn't someone who intends to be short term enlistment." Jenny sat down and took Sylvia's hand, patting it, "Listen to me. I mean it Sylvia. You haven't been out and about much. Your Hoosier outlook is not ready for such a big leap. Enjoy school and learn from those around you. If you are still unable to lose that itch you have for Ron, watch some of the mixed couples. You know we have them here at IU. Watch them and learn from them. Talk to them even, but don't tell your parents about Ron until you are really sure that is a battle you want to fight. It is a big deal in this country right now. It may not be someday, but right now, it is. You might even get by with being married in a big city, but here in smalltown Indiana..... Shoot! The KKK would find your home to be an easy mark. If you think all the stories you read in the paper and see on the news just happen in the south, You. Are. Wrong. It happens here in Indiana too."

Sylvia went into the kitchenette of their university apartment and put some ice cubes in two glasses then poured in the new "diet drink" from Coca Cola, Tab. She handed a glass to Jenny as entered the small living room again. "Here," she said as she extended her hand and the drink. "I know you may be right. I take that back, I know you are right. I just have never had such an attraction. I know he is Negro. I know that right now is a difficult time for them in our country, but Jenny, I don't see him as a Negro. I know his skin is dark, but all I see is a wonderful man who happens to have darker skin than mine. Why is that so awful?"

Jenny gave a deep sigh. "It isn't, Sylvia. I do understand. When we were in DC, in the apartment, playing cards I didn't see the difference either. When we were out walking around though, we got stared at. And the stares weren't pleasant. The only reason we didn't have more trouble was the way that Ron kind of seems like he was behind us rather than with us. I think he did that to protect you and me. I like Ron. I understand that we don't choose who we love, love chooses us, but sometimes we can't act on that. It could be dangerous for you both. What happens when you have children? That is another thing to consider. Would they be accepted by either one of their families or society in general?" She sat the drink on the coffee table and got up to give Sylvia a big hug. "You know I will always be your friend, don't you?"

Sylvia gave a weak smile and shook her head.

The girls' classes kept them busy, but not so busy that Sylvia could not write to Ron. She knew that in doing that, she was letting herself fall more deeply in love with him. Perhaps if she had simply thrown herself in her work and accepted dates when someone asked her out, she could have molded her life differently, but she knew her heart.

Dear Ron,

I know it has only been two weeks since I met you, but I hope we can correspond with each other. Classes started and I am looking forward to the year and beginning my career at the Lab School here at IU. They get us in a classroom as soon as they can so that we really know what we are getting into. I know some colleges and universities don't have that option and a student will get to their student teaching before they realize they don't want to teach. I think that would be terrible to go to school for four years or more then decide you don't want to do the very thing you have trained to do. Do you ever feel that way at the Academy? I know you had opportunities in DC when you mentored Brad, but did that help you decide what you want to do after you graduate? Does the Navy let you have some control over what you do or where you are stationed?

I watch the news, and I am so disheartened. I do not like this war, and I have some friends from high school who have enlisted. I pray for them every night and hope they come home safe and sound. I would worry more if you or Brad had to go to Vietnam or anywhere there is such harsh fighting. I pray for you both every night as I toss and turn before I finally go to sleep.

I have a question for you, Ron. Do you know of any mixed race couples? After I got back here on campus, I have noticed several couples who are dating that are from different countries and different cultures. It does not seem like they have a problem, but I don't know them well enough to ask them about it. It has been a point of curiosity since we met, I will admit. I don't see you as a Negro, Ron. I will treasure our friendship greatly, but my feelings go deeper for you than they ever have for anyone else. I don't want promises, but I don't think I could stand it if we couldn't be friends. Please, let's write and get to know each other better as friends. I truly believe there is a plan and a purpose for all of us. I don't question that, I only try to follow my heart.

Love,

Sylvia

Dearest Sylvia,

I am so glad you wrote. I certainly want to continue to get to know you better. I am not much of a writer. I am a much better talker. I have thought about you quite a bit since you left. I am back at the Academy and no longer see Brad daily, so getting to know you through letters will work out very well.

You asked about our choices. I am going into the administrative side of things. It will give me the momentum I need to propel my career through quick promotions. I have worked fairly extensively with war strategies and combat history. That will, hopefully, queue me up for promotions. Right now, in this country and in the military, being a black man will work to my advantage. I will give them more than they will get from anyone else. Now, as to where they will station me, I have no control over that. I can place a request, but they will send me wherever I am needed. With my strategic studies, I have to be realistic and understand that they will be sending me, most probably, to Vietnam.

We are getting a lot of instruction about the kind of warfare we are facing in that arena, so I would imagine that is where they are planning on sending most of the graduates of the Academy for the next couple of years. I only hope the conflict is over quickly. We have a good man in President Kennedy. He had a lot of experience, himself, in the Pacific. I hope the advisors don't talk him into extending time in the area for too long. If they do that, it is a conflict we will not win.

Enough about me, tell me about some of your experiences in the Lab School you mentioned. I bet those kids light up when you enter the room, I know I would. Like you, I think we can get to know each other better for the time being. I am sure I will come home with Brad at some point in time and we can discuss our future in more detail. You take care of yourself, sweetie.

Love to you,
Ron

THE UNIMAGINABLE HAPPENS but life goes on.

Ron was sitting in his room studying for finals that were to be held the next week when his roommate burst in, "Did you hear!! Oh, my God!! What will happen? I can't believe it."

Ron put his book down and looked over, "What?" He knew his easygoing roommate would not be this upset unless something major had happened.

"The President, Ron. Someone shot President Kennedy. Let's go!" He left the room to go to the commons area on the dorm floor. As the two entered, all of the guys on the floor were glued to the news. Walter Cronkite was visibly shaken as he reported that the President had just been pronounced dead. Johnson would be sworn in within a few moments aboard Air Force One.

During the next few days the entire country operated on auto-pilot. Brad had been in touch and Ron made certain that he called Sylvia. Brad had told Ron that he would be going home for Christmas and invited Ron to spend a few days in Indiana if he could. Ron needed to see Sylvia. The reality of the hate that would inspire the assassination of a

President along with the growing civil unrest was causing Ron to want to hold Sylvia close and protect her from all of it. He knew deep down, however, that their love for each other would only lead to more heartache for them both.

Ron met up with Brad to watch the procession that carried Kennedy's body from the Capitol Rotunda to St. Matthew's for the requiem Mass. Neither of them would ever be able to forget the veiled face of Jacqueline Kennedy with their daughter Caroline and a young John Jr. saluting his father's casket.

Before the funeral took place, another tragedy occurred. Lee Harvey Oswald, the man accused of assassinating President John Kennedy, was when he was murdered by Jack Ruby in full view of television cameras in the basement of the Dallas Police station. Another nail in the coffin of America. How much strife could the country withstand? It was a question that Ron found himself thinking of often. There were theories flying about both the assassination as well as the killing of Oswald.

Plans changed for the two young men and therefore, Ron and Brad got together over the holidays at Ron's parents' home in Virginia. Neither of them had time for a trip to Indiana, and Ron felt that not seeing Sylvia might be good. He had called Sylvia on occasion, and, while it was difficult to end the conversation, he still had misgivings about continuing the relationship.

Back Home Again in Indiana

"Hey, MOM!" Brad yelled as he went in the back door of his home in Bloomington.

"Brad, it is good to see you!" his mother said as she rushed to hug her son, only to have him put his arms around her and give her the biggest hug she had received since he left. "You put me down," she laughed.

"Oh, Mom, it is good to see you. Is Dad out in the shop?"

"Nope," Sam Carver said as he came through the back door and gave his son a big hug. "How ya doin', son?" he asked as he looked over at Ron. "Who's your friend?"

"This is my good buddy, Ron, "

"Ron Michaels, sir," Ron said as he shook Sam's hand. "It is nice meeting you, sir. Thanks for the invitation to visit."

"Any time, son," he said as he shook his hand and put his left hand on Ron's right shoulder. "Any friend of Brad's is always welcome here."

"Something sure smells good, Mom. If I was guessing, I would say meatloaf."

"You would be guessing right. I fixed enough that I invited the Greenes over. Sylvia is home this week and I thought it might be a good way for you kids to catch up."

Ron and Brad exchanged glances. Both thinking that this was too good to be true. It would be an easy conversation because everyone knew that Sylvia had met Ron a year ago when she and Jenny had gone to DC near the end of summer vacation.

Meanwhile, Sylvia took the pies out of the oven and sat them on top of the stove to cool. Her mother and dad were running late so she decided to go over and let the Carvers know that they would all be a little late. The back door was open and she stumbled on the door jamb as she entered the Carver's kitchen. There in front of her, with smiles on their faces, were Brad and Ron. She ran over and hugged them both at the same time, hoping it would not raise questions she didn't want to answer from either set of parents. "You dogs!!!" she laughed. "Brad why didn't you let me know you were here already? I wasn't expecting you guys until tomorrow."

Brad gave her a special hug and kiss on the cheek as he replied, "Well, sweet cheeks, we got an earlier plane. Don't expect me to tell you everything."

She grinned then held out her hand to Ron, "Ron, it is so good to see you again." It was all she could do to contain the shiver that shaking his hand sent up her arm and onto the core of her as her nipples tightened.

He smiled his easy smile and nodded, "It is good to see you again, too, Sylvia. I hope you can invite Jenny over and we can continue that game of euchre you Hoosiers seem so fond of."

Sylvia laughed her soft laugh, and Ron felt his body respond to the lilt in her voice. "She was invited over tomorrow night, so we are set for euchre."

The group sat and comfortably discussed the country's events, asking Ron questions of curiosity as the news applied to him as a black man. The term Negro had fallen out of favor and had been replaced with "black."

A couple of nights later, the group had decided to go to a movie in town. All four were avid Alfred Hitchcock fans, so *Marnie* was their only choice. *Mary Poppins* had received some good reviews, and if they decided to go across town to another theatre, that might be the next one. Everything was going very well until the group left to go the a nearby pizza house after the show.

"That Hitchcock can really direct a story to keep you on the edge of your seat," Jenny shivered.

"*Rear Window* is my favorite," said Sylvia.

"I think mine is *North by Northwest*," said Ron.

"Oh, I loved that one too," Sylvia chimed in.

"Let's face it, gang. We could do a Hitchcock marathon and enjoy every one of them equally," Brad stated.

The group grabbed some menus and went to a back booth. Jenny scooted in and before Sylvia could slide in after her, Brad scooted in first. "You go over there, sweetie," he said, nodding to the other side of the booth. Ron stood waiting for Sylvia, who scooted in and he followed.

The waitress came up with a tray with four glasses of water. She put the tray down on the table quickly when she saw Sylvia sitting next to Ron. Her face flushed and she removed the glasses of water, then, taking the tray, she turned and left. She came back in a few moments with her order pad, asking what they would like to eat. After an order for a large supreme pizza and sodas were placed, the couples discussed the waitress's strange behavior.

In about twenty minutes, the pizza they ordered was brought out by a man who appeared to be the manager. It was in a box ready to be taken home. "Sir," Brad said, "We were going to eat here."

"Yeah, kid. You were planning on it, but it would be in your best interest to just take the pizza home. We usually have some late night customers that don't take kindly to the mixing of the race groups. That's not my take, but I don't want to be calling the cops when a fight breaks out. Come back during the daytime and I will make you another pizza "on the house.""

The foursome looked at each other and got out of the booth and readied themselves to go on home.

As they were getting ready to get in the car, a turquoise and white '57 Chevy pulled up behind them. Brad and Ron hurried the girls in Brad's car and quickly got in the car and left as a group of guys got out of the Chevy.

"I think we may just have escaped an incident," Brad said, giving a deep sigh of relief.

"Yeah, I think so too," said Ron. He turned and looked at Sylvia who was sitting behind Brad as he drove. He hated seeing the sad look on her face. She, too, understood what could have happened if those guys had seen them sitting in the booth together. It was their reality, and Ron decided then and there that nothing more was going to happen between them that would cause her harm.

The rest of Brad and Ron's time in Indiana was spent having a good time. They laughed and enjoyed more movies, more pizza, and more conversation. The conversation was light and bright and Ron made certain he and Sylvia were never alone together. He had been taking long cold showers since the first evening she tripped into the Carver's kitchen.

Sylvia had tossed and turned every night, dreaming of Ron. She had tried to get him by himself but had failed on every front. Jenny had tried to get Brad to help her get something out of the trunk one evening, but Ron had insisted that he go out too, in case Brad needed help. She knew he was trying to avoid intimate conversation with her, but she had so much she wanted to tell him. She was not ready to confess how much she loved him, but she wanted him to know that she was not going anywhere with anyone while she was in college. She wanted him to know that as he got closer and closer to overseas deployment.

The day came for Brad and Ron to leave. Jenny and Sylvia were driving them to the airport. The girls had a plan that they felt was foolproof so that Sylvia could get a few minutes alone with Ron. It would take choreographed moves on their part, but they felt they had worked it out the best they could. While waiting for the bus, Jenny feigned a fall. Brad rose to go to her and so did Ron. Sylvia quickly stepped in toward Ron, grabbed his hand, and pulled him around the corner of the station into the alley and wrapped her arms around his neck and pressed her body into his. His arms automatically circled her waist, and he pulled her close to him as their lips found each other. Their tongues explored each other, and Sylvia moaned as she felt Ron begin to harden. She paused and put her head on his shoulder giving a sigh of contentment. "You take care of yourself, Ron," she said as she stepped away from him. "I know you have been avoiding this, but I couldn't let you get away without one kiss."

As she looked up at him, he reached out and pulled her close to him as he once again took her lips, circled her waist and let his hands roam down and pull her ass toward him. "One day, Sweetie, we will do more than kiss. I promise you that. Keep writing me, please."

"You can look forward to it," she said with tears in her eyes as they left the alley and went back into the station to continue the wait for the bus that would take Ron back to finish his work and receive his orders. Brad had a bit of a break since he was a couple of years behind Ron, but after the discussions about the war, it appeared that President Johnson was escalating the fighting and it was not going to be the brief engagement that had once been thought.

Ron's Deployment

A Trip to Remember

When school was out the spring of 1964, Jenny and Sylvia headed to Washington, DC to visit Brad and Ron. Sylvia's parents felt secure that Brad would take good care of the girls as they all went to Annapolis to see Ron graduate from the Academy.

"You don't think we are doing the wrong thing, do you?" Linda Greene asked her husband, Brian.

"I am not sure we are doing the right thing. You see the way she lights up when Ron's name is even mentioned. When he was here for a visit, the chemistry was noticeable. Do I think we are doing them any favors? No. The world is not ready for the kind of love they have, but I know if someone had told me I couldn't marry you, I would have tried just that much harder," he replied as he leaned over and kissed his wife.

"Yes, but you and I never had to fight what they are going to have to fight."

"Sweetheart, it will make them or break them. If their love is strong, it will survive. Ron is as fine a man as I could hope for Sylvia. She is level-headed, and she isn't going to do anything rash."

"I hope you're right," Linda sighed. Although Indiana was not one of them, there were still several states in the United States where interracial marriages were actually illegal.

Linda sat and thought back to some of the recent facts and information she had come across since realizing that Sylvia was falling in love with a Negro. Linda and Brian neither held any prejudice against someone because of their race, but they were not ostriches, thinking the problem would go away if they just ignored it.

In the 1920s five million Americans joined the Ku Klux Klan, and Hoosiers were the most politically powerful Klan in the country. Between one-fourth and one-third of native-born white Hoosier males had joined the group, and at its peak in 1925 it had a membership greater than the Methodist church, Indiana's largest denomination. While the Klan was no longer a visible political presence like it was in the twenties, it still existed. What people did not realize as the Klan's political presence faded was that a social presence took its place. It was not directed only at the black population; it also targeted Catholics, Jews, immigrants, and feminists. Indeed, the Indiana of the 1960s was deemed to be the northernmost Southern state in the United States because of some of the overall social views that had been passed along for the last fifty years of its statehood.

========================

"Mom, Dad, these are our friends, Sylvia and Jenny," Ron said as he introduced the girls to his parents.

"You are just as lovely as Ron said you were," Amelia Michaels remarked as she pulled Sylvia into a hug. "And Brad, I think you found yourself a beauty too."

"Thank you, Ma'am," Sylvia said as she blushed.

"Thanks," Jenny echoed.

"Hey there folks, I have us some seats saved. We had better get to them." James and Amelia had been told about Sylvia after Ron got back from his visit to Indiana. He did not want to keep his parents in the dark, but James was a bit surprised that Amelia was so forthcoming. She was a good judge of character, and evidently she had made up her mind quickly about Sylvia Greene and her potential as a future daughter-in-law.

Amelia's sister had married a white man and moved to Toronto because of the extreme prejudice they had been subject to. She worried about her only son and his lovely girlfriend. Sylvia appeared to be a dear girl, intelligent and caring. She was all a mother could hope her son would find, but not everyone felt that way. More than once she had looked over at James observing the two young people with a bit of a wrinkle between his brows. She went over and locked her arm through his. "You do realize that all the worrying in the world won't change anything that is in the future, don't you?"

He reached his right hand over and patted Amelia's hand as it was hooked around his arm. "Yes, ma'am, you are surely correct, but I just wonder what those two kids were thinking."

Amelia just laughed. "Like they had a choice. You don't choose love; it chooses you."

"Very true," he agreed as he continued patting her hand.

New Experiences

Washington, DC was an exciting place for Sylvia and Jenny. They felt comfortable in the city. Brad was continuing his education at the Academy while Ron accepted a temporary assignment as a recruiter for the Navy. His classic appearance as a Naval junior officer impressed high school men who were looking to find their identity in helping keep the world safe from Communism. Ron was a very successful recruiter, garnering more inductees in one month than the last recruiter had in three months. The Navy felt he was right where he needed to be until they decided otherwise. Sylvia couldn't have been happier. Jenny went back home and Sylvia stayed. Brad was in Annapolis so Ron sublet his DC apartment. There were two bedrooms, and Sylvia moved in certain that she and Ron would not cross boundaries they had both agreed to.

Ron rolled over in his bed. He was a hard as a rock just knowing Sylvia was across the hall, in her pajamas, with the door unlocked. He got out of bed wearing only the boxer shorts he slept in and decided to go get a drink of water before he went back to bed. He saw a dim light in the kitchen and rounded the corner to see Sylvia getting the milk out of the refrigerator.

CRASH! The milk slipped from her hands and spilled all over the floor. "Oh, Ron, you scared me to death. What are you doing up?"

"Probably the same thing you are. I can't sleep either."

"You know, this probably isn't a very good idea," Sylvia said.

"What? Milk in the middle of the night? Why not?" Ron asked.

She swatted at him, "No, silly. I probably need to pack up and go back home for the summer. We aren't going to be able to keep our hands off of each other if I stay."

"Well, who says we need to?"

"Ron, we agreed there would be no sex this summer."

"Yeah," he sighed, "We did agree. But, we could play around a bit."

Sylvia bit her lip. She had been thinking the same thing, but she wasn't sure what that would even mean. She had dated, but she had gone no further than kissing with the boys she dated in high school. Ron was the only man who had ever made her feel like she needed more. "I am not sure that is a good idea."

"Well, Hell!" Ron exclaimed, "I'm not either, but I want you so badly." He took her hand and placed it over his erection, and her instinct was to wrap her hand around it and step toward him.

"You are so big. I didn't know men got that big."

"How much fooling around have you done, Sweetie?" he asked.

"Well," she said, blushing, "not much."

Ron pulled her to him in a gentle hug. "I am not going to do more than hold you right now, but Sylvia, I ache at night for you. Every night. I want to hold you and taste you and get inside you in the worst way, but we are not going to do anything that we don't both decide to do when we decide to do it. I don't want you to leave, but I can't guarantee I won't try to get you to let me give you some pleasure without the final act of intercourse."

"You can do that?" she asked with amazement in her voice.

"Yes, I can, but I am not going to tonight. We are just going to lay down in my bed and fall asleep..... Together."

Ron took her hand, and they went into his bedroom. She took her robe off and climbed into bed. "Oh, dear Jesus in heaven above," Ron moaned as he watched her go hands and knees into bed with her pear-shaped ass pointed toward him. His shorts tented as he began to get hard. "I will be back in a second, I have to take a quick shower," he said as he turned and headed down the hall to the bathroom. He closed the door, got into the shower and quickly put one hand out on the side of the shower stall and pumped his cock with the other hand dreaming it was pumping into her beautiful body. He shot a thick stream of cum as he whispered her name. One day she would be his and one day he would be inside her, worshiping her body instead of standing here like a foolish teenage kid jacking off.

===========================

Sylvia got a part time job easily that summer. She worked at the Southeast Neighborhood Library as a research assistant and enjoyed it immensely. She and Ron settled into a comfortable routine but rarely went out in public until July of that year. Lyndon Johnson signed into law the Civil Rights Act of 1964 which prohibited segregation in public places. The rest of the summer, Ron and Sylvia were able to enjoy their summer more freely than before even though they were both very aware of the contemptuous stares they often received when they were out together.

Their private life was one that allowed their friendship to grow over the summer. Neither of them quite knew how they were going to go back to their lives when the summer ended and threw themselves into enjoying the moments they had available to them right then. They laughed over the hijacks of Wilbur and *Mr. Ed* then caught up on the news as they watched *Face the Nation* on Sunday mornings over omelettes. The routine they enjoyed and the evenings spent in each other's arms were becoming more comfortable.

Sylvia found it more and more difficult to keep her hands off of Ron, and one night in August, she woke up in the middle of the night to find Ron's hands on her belly pulling her closer to him. She felt his hardness and sighed as her body responded to his touch. He kissed the back of her neck and nuzzled the area behind her ear where her neck and shoulders met, murmuring into her ear how much he loved her. Sylvia rolled over and slipped her arms around his waist and lifted her right leg up over his hip and fit herself into his heat. She had been in the habit of wearing only panties and a t-shirt to bed, an outfit that was not nearly thick enough for Ron to miss the moistness between her legs or the pebbled nipples that pushed into him.

"Sylvia."

"Shhhh……" she said as she pushed her warm moist core closer to his hard cock. Her body began responding, and Ron responded by reaching to cup her ass and pull her closer. "Ahhhhhh…" she moaned as they began rhythmically responding to the heat they created together. It was not long before Sylvia's body exploded with pleasure as Ron watched her face as her eyes widened, looking into his with adoration. "Oh, Ron, that was wonderful," she murmured as she rested her head on his shoulder.

Ron throbbed, knowing he could not move away until Sylvia fell asleep. He knew if she were to touch him he would erupt instantly. He just wanted to enjoy the closeness regardless of the pain he was feeling. He felt her hand move down his back and lower to his hips as it came around to grasp him. "Let me give you pleasure," she said as she began taking long strokes. He pushed into her hand for only a minute until the pent up love and emotion was sexually released onto her shirt. He pulled her closer and the two drifted off only to awaken the next morning and shower together exploring each other again. Being this close yet not being able to be inside her was getting more unbearable for them both.

"Ron," Sylvia began, "we really need to discuss last night."

"Please don't tell me you are sorry for what we did, or ashamed."

"Oh, my God! No. I enjoyed it like nothing I have experienced. I enjoyed it on many different levels. The physical release, I didn't realize it could be so intense, and the love and closeness we have experienced until now was just tripled. No, I want to let you know that while I don't think I am ready for actual 'sex,' I don't know if I can sleep in the same bed knowing that pleasure is available to us both and yet denying it."

"Well, as you discovered last night, we can enjoy each other without penetration," Ron smiled.

"I know, but, I don't know how long that will be able to satisfy me. I wanted you inside me so much last night, Ron, it made me ache."

"I know, Baby. Why do you think I have been taking so many showers? I go in there and relieve the pressure. I want you so much. I think about you all the time and what it will be like when I finally get to push into that hot, tight body of yours." He pulled her over on top of his lap. As he cupped her butt and pulled her closer, she felt his hardness and threw her head back as she slid closer to that heat.

"Make me come, Ron. I need you to make me come now."

Ron leaned in and began sucking on her nipples through the t-shirt she had put on after their shower. "Is this good?'

"Mmmmm... oh, Ron. Don't stop. I need you." She began a rhythm of moving against his hard dick, and he reached down between them into her panties and slid a finger into her slick folds. "Ahhhhhh!" she squirmed "Oh, my God. Ron, I am coming. I am coming." She picked up her movements and Ron added another finger and pressed against her clit in a movement that caused her to unravel and continue to pump and pump on his hand.

"Oh, my God… Ron… don't stop. Please don't stop… I don't think this is over. Her movements got more primal as they continued the pumping rhythm. Ron reached deeply into her and found the spongy area and continued to move his thick finger around and around as his other hand found her clit and tweaked it between his thumb and forefinger, milking it as his fingers pounded her. Sylvia experienced flashes of fireworks behind her closed eyes as she screamed, "OH, GOD, Ron… Ron…. AHHHHHHH!"

Ron slowed his movements as he felt the pulsing around his fingers begin to slow, and he murmured softly in her ear, "Easy, Baby, easy. Just enjoy it; enjoy it." He brought her down from a high that he had never seen from a woman. While he was hard as stone, all he could do was watch her enjoy the experience, knowing that this would be the first of many times they would be taken to heaven and back until the time came for Sylvia to go back to Indiana and finish school. It was a subject they did not talk about, but it loomed over them every morning when they awoke.

Summer of '64

The racial situation in the summer of 1964 had been legislated, but the hearts of people had not changed. While steps had been taken legally to ensure rights to the black population, not all areas were affected. Interracial marriage remained against the law in some states. There were more and more private clubs formed with charters that kept them segregated, which was entirely legal. The laws only applied to public spaces, not private ones, so the tension did not go away.

At the end of August, just one week before Sylvia was to leave, Ron received orders in response to the attack on the USS Maddox in the Gulf of Tonkin earlier that month. He was going to be sent to the area as a junior strategist and would be staged, for the time being, in Thailand. He was expected to leave in forty-eight hours. Sylvia made arrangements with Ron's parents for them to come and see their son off, then she wept and wept over knowing that he would be so far away.

James and Amelia arrived about three hours after Sylvia had called them. Ron had left the arrangements to her since he had to be at headquarters to run the rigorous tests, both physical and mental, that the Navy required of those officers assigned to Southeast Asia. James paced while Amelia and Sylvia had a serious discussion about Ron. Sylvia was much more comfortable talking to Amelia than she was her own mother when it came to her relationship with Ron. Amelia's family and James's family both had members from different cultures and ethnicities, and the conversation was one which Amelia had before with members of her own family. She loved Sylvia, and while she knew it would not be easy, she realized the depth of love her son felt for this beautiful soul.

The War Interferes

Sylvia wrote Ron every day letting him know of her experiences during her student teaching. She shared with him her excitement over her first contract in Elliotsville, a small town close to Bloomington. Her letters were filled with love and plans for their life when the war ended and he was back home. Ron digested her letters and read them over more than once as he laid in his bed and ached to have her in his arms. He wrote back as often as he could. He knew he was a coward. Life in Thailand was much easier than it would have been in Vietnam, but there was much he could not tell her.

Ron had been sent to Saigon for two weeks, and during that time, he had left letters with his buddies to send to Sylvia telling her of his love for her. He could not reveal that he was on a classified assignment to plan strategies with the leaders of South Vietnam. In the course of those two weeks, he had seen more carnage in the areas of engagement than he had thought was possible in such a small country. He realized the scope of the war and did not want any disenchantment to reach his love. He also had realized before he left that there would be much more scrutiny of his mail from Saigon, and he didn't want to upset any of his family if they were to find out that he was in an area much more dangerous than Thailand.

"You old hound dog!" Ron heard in a familiar voice as he turned around and saw Brad.

The two men hugged and slapped each other one the back. "Let me buy you a drink," Ron said, astounded that Brad was standing there in front of him. "How on God's green earth did you end up here?" he asked.

"They need someone with my skills," Brad said with a shrug.

Ron's eyes narrowed, "Oh, yeah? And how does seducing a *gai giaug ho* in this area qualify you for a position?"

Brad slapped a hand on Ron's left shoulder and said, "Let's get us a table in the back and we can talk." The young waitress came over and asked for their order. The two men, who were obviously American soldiers, were fair game for all of the *gai giaug ho* just because they were Americans. The women saw it as their way of getting out of the country. If they could get one of the soldiers to get them pregnant, then their children would be Americans. It was a prize they all attempted to win. Both men looked at the young woman with compassion rather than the disdain many viewed them with. She had obviously found a man who was willing to bed her, but Brad and Ron's look indicated she would probably be one of the hundreds who was used and would be left behind to raise a child who was American but would never be recognized as such; instead, the child would only suffer because of it.

"Poor girl," Ron said with a shake of his head after she left.

"Well, she took a gamble and lost. It happens."

Ron looked at his friend. A comment like that was not one he recognized from Brad. "What crawled up your ass and died?" he asked.

"This fucking war is a mistake. It is a disaster. We need to get the hell out. Do you know what is going on, what is REALLY going on?"

"Wellllll... I thought I did," Ron drawled. "Are you going to tell me something else? I thought we were keeping Communism at bay and helping the South Vietnamese get out from under the Communist aggression of the north."

"Yeah, that much of the propaganda is true, to a certain extent." Brad had been leaning closer to Ron and leaned back as the waitress appeared with their drinks. *"Lam on doi mot lat!"* Brad said as he pulled out a ten-dollar bill and handed the girl.

She smiled and her face lit up, *"Cam on rat nhieu."* She bowed and left the two to their drinks.

"Crash course?" Ron asked.

"Yep. I need to be able to speak the language and understand it for where I am going."

"Can you tell me where that would be?"

"No, but you are a smart man; you can probably guess. Hey, changing the subject. I get a letter from Sylvia about every week. You two still together?"

Ron rubbed his hand over his forehead. "Yeah, we are. I hear from her about every day unless the mail gets fucked up, which is pretty often. She is something else. I hope when we get done fighting this goddamned war I can go back to my own country and be able to marry her without eyes looking me over like I am not good enough for a white girl."

The men changed the conversation and Ron bought the next round of drinks, tipping generously as Brad had, knowing that between the two of them, the young woman could live for several weeks if she got to keep her tips. When she came around for the third time, Brad took her aside and the two talked. He reached in his pocket and brought out a folded bill, pressed it in her hand, and put his finger to his lips in the universal "Don't tell anyone" sign. She nodded, gave a small smile and left, tucking the bill in the waist of her pants.

"She will be able to live a couple of months on that, won't she?" Ron asked.

"If she is frugal, probably. She agreed to keep her eyes and ears open for me. She just became an asset."

"Isn't that a little dangerous for both of you?" Ron asked.

"It can be, but since she is pregnant, most of her own people pay no attention to her or anything she does. She has become invisible."

"So," Ron said, looking intently at Brad and trying to gauge his level of involvement. "Tell me more about this Air America. I thought it was simply a commercial airlines that uses retired American pilots for the most part to deliver goods and people to this area of the world where other commercial airlines don't want to come these days. Is there more?"

"That is what I have been sent here to find out. They appear legitimate, but there is a government watchdog group that is getting whispers that it may actually be a black ops arm of the CIA with unlimited funds and a darker objective of smuggling. People, drugs, arms, in and out."

Ron said nothing but looked into his drink as he turned the glass in his hands. He slowly responded, "If that is the case, does that mean that people within our own government are working to extend the war rather than shorten it by creating a false dependence on the economics of those items?"

Brad looked at him without answering for a moment so that Ron could let it sink in. That was exactly what it meant but Brad couldn't say it without betraying the confidentiality clauses he had sworn to.

The two men finished their drinks and left the bar, going back to the hotel where he was staying, and Ron invited Brad in for a while. Brad took out his "bug smasher" that had been issued for him to detect listening devices and as he ran it around the obvious places he found three devices that he removed and placed in water. Ron could not believe that he was being listened in on and couldn't figure out why. As they discussed this, Brad informed Ron of the plans in Washington to step up the war effort.

Over a year had passed since Ron had been stateside, and he had hoped his deployment would be shortened by his time in Saigon, but it looked as though that would not be the case. He was being tracked and that meant that the work he was doing was being monitored by the enemy. After talking to Brad he wondered if it was being tracked by his own government. Only time would tell. He was just relieved that he had left plenty of letters Sylvia to be mailed to Sylvia on a weekly basis.

Sylvia Left Wondering

Sylvia sensed that something was a bit off with Ron's letters. She was used to asking him questions, and within a couple of weeks at least, the answers would come or he would refer to something she had said in some way. These letters she was getting were almost as if he had someone else writing them.She knew that often men left letters with others when they went on dangerous missions, she only hoped and prayed that he was safe. It had been a year, now almost a year and a half, since she had seen him. It was the winter of 1966, and while his letters continued to professed his love for her, they contained very few anecdotes about life in Thailand. She knew from Brad that they had seen each other, but Brad had not mentioned where, and Ron had not mentioned it at all. The only thing she could figure out was that he had been sent elsewhere and was not able to tell her where. She communicated with his parents, and they had said nothing to her, so she did not mention it to them

.   Thinking back over Ron's letters, Sylvia recalled that troops had been sent into an area of intensive bombing in early March 1965. She had sensed concern on Ron's part about how this development fit into what he was hearing over there. He had still been in Thailand then. She also knew that he had been temporarily sent to both Laos and Cambodia to assist the French troops still in the area who were planning six-month exit strategies, yet more troops were coming in. It really didn't make sense to him or to her when he shared it with her. He avoided specifics like that most of the time, but she found it comforting when he did share those bits because she felt like he was really beginning to think of them as partners in the reality of their life.

Like most families, there was a lot of tension as the war continued to escalate. It had reached the point that President Johnson had to send more troops in or withdraw completely and discontinue United States involvement. The decision was made to bomb Hanoi and Haiphong, the two most populated cities in North Vietnam. The war photojournalists sent pictures of civilian bombings, and, as the devastation continued, many Americans began or continued protesting the involvement of the United States in a war that was beginning to look like no one could win.

By the beginning of 1967 Ron's letters once again reflected anecdotes and information abou this life, and Sylvia was relieved to know he was indeed safe and sound in Bangkok once more. In May 1967 Ron began letting Sylvia know that he had been informed that he was in line to be sent home. The families became excited at this news, but his return date kept being pushed back later and later, which made Sylvia grow more irritable every day. How much could young people in the country be expected to give of their lives for a war that was not just and served no purpose?

Back in the States

Thanksgiving Surprise

Sylvia was in the kitchen brewing the coffee when the doorbell rang early on Thanksgiving morning of 1967. She pulled her robe together and tied it around her waist. "I'll get it," she yelled up the stairs to her parents.

When she opened the door, she took one look at Ron's brown eyes and promptly fainted in his arms. He scooped her up and hurriedly took her over to the couch, calling upstairs for her parents. Linda and Brian rushed down, and Linda quickly went to the bathroom for a cool white cloth to put on Sylvia's forehead.

"Well, son," Brian remarked, "you certainly know how to make an entrance."

"I wanted to surprise her," Ron said as he backed away so her mother could tend to her.

"I would say you accomplished that," said Linda.

"Ron??" said Sylvia, "Is it really you?"

"The one and only, Sylvia. I love you so much," he said as he bent down to kiss her. He stood again and handed Linda the wash cloth.

Linda took the cloth and looked over to Brian with a raised eyebrow and they turned to leave.

"Good to have you home, Ron," said Linda gently pressing a kiss to his cheek.

"Thank you , Ma'am," he replied.

"I think you need to call me Linda," she said smiling as she turned to join her husband.

"Oh, Ron." Sylvia sat up as Ron got down on his knee near the couch. She wrapped her arms around his neck and pulled herself into his embrace. She leaned up to press her lips to his as they kissed each other intimately. He gave a sigh as he felt her body through the civilian clothes he had donned as soon as he got to town and secured a motel room. He could sense her body's response to his and could hardly wait to get her to himself. He knew that he could not take her from her family today, but as soon as possible after the festivities and meal of the day, he would find a time to whisk her away and ask her to marry him.

The couple was in for another great surprise when the Carvers came over to join them and had Brad in tow. The threesome hugged and hugged, knowing that there were so many families whose loved ones were still where they had both been only a few short weeks ago and that some families would never see their loved ones again.

The families laughed and lamented and had serious discussions and off the wall humor as they gave thanks for all their blessings. Brad and Ron had a chance to drink a beer together in the family room as Sylvia helped her mother clear the table.

"Why don't you go on over there with Ron and Brad," she encouraged her daughter.

"No, not right now. They seem to be in a serious discussion, and it has been a while since they have seen each other too. Mom, Ron has a room at a motel here in town. He said that he would like for me to spend the night. I am going to, and I don't want to lie to you and dad. We were together during the summer three years ago, and even though we have corresponded for three years, we need to reconnect and see if we still love each other like we did after that summer."

"I don't think you have to worry about that, Honey. He couldn't take his eyes off you during dinner. I just worry about what you kids will be going through if you decide to get married. You know, marriage isn't easy at best, and you have some big rocks thrown in front of you."

"We know that, Mom. We saw that every time we went out when we were in DC. It will be okay. It really will."

The two hugged each other, and when Sylvia looked over at Ron, he looked up and smiled at her with such love that she knew their feelings for each other were still there.

Sylvia left her mother's hug and walked over to Brad and Ron. She gave Brad a big hug and asked him if he had been keeping in touch with Jenny.

"I did for while, but I think she met someone she really wanted to get to know better so her letters dropped off. She would still write once in awhile but I haven't heard in almost a year. How is she?"

"Well, she did meet someone and they got married. Right now she is about a month away from having her first baby."

"What do you know! That is great. Does she still live in the area?"

"Yes, and I am sure she would love to hear from you. You treated her well, Brad. She always asks if I have heard from you when I see her. I have her number if you want to call."

"Oh," he said as he stretched after having such a big meal, "I am not sure that would be a good idea. Her husband might get the idea that we were more than just friends."

Sylvia and Ron both looked at Brad and grinned. There had been more than simple friendship, but neither of them were going to call him on it. Brad grinned back, "Well, you know what I mean," and they all laughed.

Brad and Ron played some ball in the driveway of the Carvers' house next door while Sylvia took a nap. She had packed an overnight bag with a sexy nightgown she had bought last time she had been in

Indianapolis. It was a beautiful blue that matched her eyes. It was trimmed around the front with white lace, had a matching stretchy lace panel set in a diamond pattern on her stomach, and flared out with a large band of lace to set off the hem. The sleeves and hem of the matching robe were also lace to match the gown. She knew that it would not be on her very long, but she felt that she and Ron both deserved the romance as long as it had been since they were together.

Ron came in the house after the guys grew too tired to continue. He was looking forward to spending the night with Sylvia. If she agreed to his plans, it would not be long before they could be together as husband and wife. He looked up as she came down the stairs with her bag in hand. Ron felt a bit awkward since he had never been in this situation. He pulled her into his arms and kissed her and told her that he was going to speak to her parents and would like for her to wait for him in the car.

Ron went into the living room and cleared his throat. "I have something I would like to ask. Would you give me permission to publically court your daughter? I love her, and, although I know our road will not always be easy, I would lay down my life for her any day of the week."

Brian and Linda looked at each other then smiled at Ron. "You have been in our prayers when you were overseas," Brian started. "We have some reservations, not for you personally, but because of the difficulty you are going to find at every corner. But we recognize you kids love each other, and we are not going to put yet another roadblock to that. Yes, you have our permission."

Ron extended his right hand to shake Brian's and said, "thank you, Sir," then turned to Linda, "ma'am." They all laughed at the formality, but as Ron turned to go they could see his body relax as he realized they were both behind their relationship.

Love Blooms

Ron turned the key in the door and opened it as Sylvia stepped inside. He gave her bag a soft toss onto the chair near the door as he reached out and pulled her into a warm embrace. "Oh," he whispered into her temple. "Do you have any idea how many nights I have thought of this moment?"

She relaxed into his embrace, returning it as she wrapped her arms around his neck and pulled her lips up to his, whispering, "probably about as many as I have," and she opened her mouth to him as they devoured each other. Their hands explored each other's body in a way that was calling back to them their last meeting.

Ron walked her backwards to the bed until the back of her knees met the bed and he eased her down. Her eyes gazed down his muscular body until they stopped at the bulge that showed beneath his belt buckle. She sat up and reached for him.

"No, no, no... not so soon, Sweetie. We have all night, and we are not going to rush this."

Sylvia chuckled, "I don't think three years is rushing. I have to feel you, Ron. Jenny had her husband buy condoms so I would have some." She reached up and ran her hand up and down his length.

Ron reached down and took her hand, "No. I am about ready to blow as it is. We need to talk for a minute."

At this, Sylvia sat back and became scared as she considered what they had to talk about after such a long separation and the tension of the day during which they could barely touch each other. She was wet at the thought of feeling him inside of her. She had ached for so long that she had begun masturbating to relieve the pressure and tension that her love and desire for Ron had provoked. She reached down and touched herself through her skirt, "I swear, Ron. If you don't do something to me, I am going to take care of it myself."

Ron realized as his cock got harder than he thought it could that they were going to have to be together before they could even get to the point of a sensible conversation. They were both wired too tightly. He had wanted their first time together to be sweet and gentle, but as he saw her rubbing herself he realized it was probably going to be hard and fast. He began unbuckling his belt as she got off the bed and they both rid themselves of their clothes. She put a strip of condoms on the nightstand near the bed as they eased down and slipped into each other's arms.

Sylvia laid back and saw Ron reach over to grab a condom, rip it open, and roll it on. He laid down beside her, and his hand reached over to her stomach and began its trail down to her warm wet folds. His finger circled her pearl peaking out from its hood. He put first one finger in and then the second as he pumped his hand in and out, pushing in deeply as she pressed her hips upward to meet his thrusts. He hit the soft spongy area, and she screamed his name as her release took hold and her muscles contracted around his fingers. He removed his fingers and her eyes widened as she moved under him taking his hard cock and directing it into her throbbing pussy. He slowly entered her and found a haven like none he had experienced. He had not partaken of the opportunities to have women in Southeast Asia, so the only relief he had felt had come from his own hand until the warmth of Sylvia wrapped around him.

"Hold on Sweet Thing," he said as he began moving in and out with the thrusts going deeper and deeper, faster and faster. As she once again began convulsing around him, he let go and came with an intensity that he had never experienced.

He rolled off of her, taking her with him as she languished nestled in his hold. She gave a deep sigh of contentment.

"I am sorry that was so fast for your first time," Ron whispered to her as he removed the condom.

"It was perfect, simply perfect, but it didn't last long enough. I might have to try that again later," she said with a mischievous grin as she snuggled closer to her. As she rubbed her hand over his hard abs, his cock twitched at the idea he could soon be in her again. She moved her hand down to wrap around his growing member and fisted her hand up and down as it continued to grow.

"Oh, God," he said. "You have the perfect touch."

"It doesn't need to be perfect," she remarked. "It just needs to be perfect for you. Take me again, Ron. I still need to feel you inside me. I have waited a lifetime to feel like I do with you."

Ron said, "I will gladly take you again, but this time it is going to be slow and sweet, and you will never again have any question about who you belong to."

"Ron, since the day I met you, I have known where home is."

"Marry me."

"What did you say?" she asked, not believing she had heard correctly.

"Marry me. As soon as we can. I love you and want to spend the rest of my life proving that to you."

"Ron, will the Navy let you marry me?"

"What do you mean? Of course the Navy will let me marry you. Why would you ask that?"

"Well," she began, "Are you going to be stationed stateside, or will you be sent overseas again? Will they let me go with you, or will I have to stay here."

"I imagine they will send me overseas again after a brief tour here. After that, I would imagine I will end up in San Diego for a while, actually."

"I want to marry you, but I don't want to go somewhere for a while when you won't be there and yet I will be far from either of our parents."

"Well, then let's just get married and not tell anyone. You can stay here until this war is over and I get a more stable assignment."

"I need to tell my parents, and yours need to know too."

"Why?"

Sylvia thought about it. She knew that her parents and his parents had no problem with the two of them being together, but she also knew that if others were aware of their interracial marriage, she could run into problems in some places and with some individuals. "You realize that if I agree to this, it is not because I am ashamed of our love, don't you?"

He nuzzled her neck. Kissing her where her neck met her shoulder, sending shivers down her spine. "Mmmmm, yeah, I don't even think we need to have that conversation."

Planning the Wedding

Sylvia woke the next morning with Ron's right arm over her waist holding her snuggly into him. She felt his erection pressing into the cleft between her cheeks and she couldn't help but wiggle back into him. "Mmm, Baby, have I told you how much I love the looks of your ass?" he said as he pushed into her and ran his hand across her hip to her ass. He rubbed and caressed her ass until his finger found the puckered opening, then he ran his rough forefinger around it.

The feeling was foreign to Sylvia but not unpleasant. She had not thought of that as being a pleasure point, but somehow she instinctively realized that any exploration of their bodies would be a thrill.

Ron removed his hand and rolled to the side as he rolled Sylvia to her back. He leaned over her and began kissing her breasts as he took one nipple into his mouth. Sylvia felt such pleasure she just decided to lay and enjoy his ministrations until she could not stand it. As he suckled her, his other hand worked the other breast and alternately ran down her torso, as far down her leg as he could reach, then back up to her breast. She reached in and took hold of his hardening cock and began stroking it slowly up and down as she felt it harden fully. The two just kept slowly working each other, knowing that the slow build up was a preface of a wonderful release. Sylvia pulled Ron on top of her as she tried to reach for a condom. Her hand moved trying to find one and finally grasped it in her hand. Putting the corner in her mouth and tearing the foil corner open, she then took the condom in her hand and rolled it onto the rock hard dick as she guided Ron into her. The two were in no hurry this morning. Hours of lovemaking the night before gave them the opportunity to engage in the most leisurely sex they had experienced. As they both came together, it was an experience not only of release but also of the deepest love they felt.

Ron and Sylvia showered separately. Sylvia had to admit that the night had left her a bit sore, and she knew if they were in that shower together, they would not leave each other alone. Besides, they needed to cool it a bit in order to discuss what would happen if they got married at this time. The Supreme Court had decided in *Loving v. Virginia* in June of that year that to deny people the right to marry based on their race was a violation of the Fourteenth Amendment. They could legally marry, but they did need to realistically face the true problems they would face on a day-to-day basis in this society. The sixties were a time of rebellion and protesting. The marches at different places in the United States the last four or five years had done much to bring attention to the problems and had helped to some degree. The problem was, and would continue to be, the hearts of the individuals.

"Ron," Sylvia began. "I'm wondering if it would be better if I moved home and stayed with my mom and dad. It would give us a chance to save some money."

"I have been thinking, too," Ron replied. "If we were to marry on a military base, you would be a documented Naval wife and would be entitled to all benefits. We could be married at Annapolis when we go visit my parents, but we would not have to tell anyone off base. What do you think? If anything happened to me, you would be fully protected by the military."

"Oh, Ron. Why do you have to talk about things like that?" Sylvia snapped. "I am not even going to think about that, but I can see that it would be better for a lot of reasons that the marriage is not totally secret. I would need to make changes to insurance and name changes. That could be done through the military, but I could continue to use my name at school as always."

The two agreed there was much to be considered, but in the meantime, they could go have blood drawn for their license. Even though this was the Friday after Thanksgiving, they could go to the hospital for a blood test. They could then go to Virginia to visit James and Amelia and take a day trip to the Naval Academy to find out what they needed to do to get married there.

Once the blood tests were taken, the couple went back to Sylvia's to eat leftovers from the huge Thanksgiving meal with them and say good bye before they left early the next morning to go to Ron's folks.

Ron had given Sylvia the ring that had been his paternal grandmother's. His mother had given it to him. It was the ring James had given her when he proposed, and the tradition was that it would remain with the woman until her first born proposed, at which time it was then taken off and given to the bride of the next generation. The two discussed whether or not they should advise Sylvia's parents of their engagement, and she felt that she would rather wait for a while before she even told them of the engagement. Not long, just maybe until next summer when she could possibly join Ron. While her parents were supportive, Sylvia felt they would feel that the two were jumping into it since they had not seen each other for three years. Sylvia and Ron both understood that viewpoint and agreed that they would tell neither set of parents for a while.

It was more difficult than they either thought it would be as they sat and ate supper that Friday evening. Sylvia had the desire to share her news with her mother and dad, but there was also a part of her that felt, for some reason, she needed to keep it hidden. She couldn't understand that feeling of foreboding that overcame her. She shrugged it off the first time she noticed it, but it became more clear to her that the Universe was trying to send her a message. She looked over at Ron and he seemed to be talking easily with her dad, so she thought maybe she was just putting potential difficulties on her path where there were none.

Linda made them promise that the next morning they would come by early before they left to get a warm breakfast as well as some sandwiches and goodies for the road. Ron and Sylvia left the Greenes' home about 7:00 am armed with food for the day. They made good time on the road to Louisville, and after that they were on I-64 eastward, which had been finished for a couple of years. There were still some areas that needed work, but it made for a rather trouble-free trip, and, with higher speed limits, the miles melted behind them.

It wa dark when Ron and Sylvia pulled in the driveway in her red 1963 Corvair at the Michaels's home. James came to greet them and helped Ron with the luggage while he told Sylvia to go on ahead of them. James wanted to have some time with Ron to let him in on some of the recent developments in Richmond. The Supreme Court decision of June that year in the *Loving v. Virginia* had not set well in some areas. While Richmond seemed to be doing okay, there were still some neighborhoods that were having problems. The interesting thing was that unfortunately, the worst of the problems were coming from the black neighborhoods like the one where Ron's parents lived. It was inhabited by a more educated populous than some of the black areas, but the racial tension was still palpable.

"Will Sylvia be safe here?" Ron asked his dad.

"I think she will be, yes, or I would have let you know to take her to DC, and we would have met you up there. I just wanted you to be on guard and attentive to the surroundings. I don't want anything to happen to either one of you. Did you give her Mommie's ring yet?" he asked his son.

"We aren't planning a wedding yet, if that is what you are asking," Ron said, avoiding the issue of engagement and partially lying about the wedding question. He felt he was okay there because they had decided, they weren't planning. He shuddered internally as he struggled with the half-truth. He and his dad had never had secrets, but this one was necessary, especially if there would be consequences if neighbors happened to find out he was going to marry a white girl.

The couple had their first taste of the local racial tension when Sylvia attended church with the Michaels family at the AME Church in Richmond that Sunday after Thanksgiving. Sylvia was a Baptist but had attended Methodist churches in Bloomington also, so she was expecting the kind of sedate church

service she was used to. In this church, there was an
outcry of "Amens" and hands held high praising God.
The singing was more robust and full of meaning,
love, and reverence. She participated in the service
as she felt she could but it lacked the exuberance
that she saw around her. There were two other white
faces, one woman and one man. She realized for the
first time how the Negroes in this country would have
felt in certain places. It was something she had
never had reason to consider. She thought of the
times that she, Brad, and Ron had gone places
where he was the only dark face. She sang and
tears ran down her cheeks as her heart ached for
him, his parents, and all of the others who were
treated so poorly by the masses. It made her sad to
think of how people often treated each other with
such disdain and hatred. She had a couple of Negro
students in her classroom. They were beginning to
ask to be called "Black" and she tried to remember to
do that. She vowed after today, she would make a
much greater effort to bridge the gap of
understanding between the white and black races.
She had never before been called to consider her
skin color as a race. She came from a place of
whiteness and did not realize how skin color would,
or could, so completely define someone. This was
the world she would be a part of. Was she strong
enough to enter Ron's world? Was their love strong
enough to endure the hatred that they would

encounter in some places? She looked over at Ron. He took her hand and kissed her fingers, tightening his hold on them. He gave a slight nod, dropped her hand, put his arm around her shoulder, then leaned over and whispered, "It will all be okay, trust me."

Looking Upward

Sylvia looked up and in that moment realized that whatever the obstructions that would be placed in front of them, they could weather the storm. No one had ever told her that life would be easy. She was fortunate that she had been given love and a great sense of moral and ethical values as she had grown up. It would serve her well as she stepped into a more diverse world than she had been living in so far in Indiana.

Her marriage to Ron was going to see her living in different places. There would be times he would be deployed overseas that she would be on a Naval base or return home to her parents. She thought about the times that she would be called upon to be a single parent when he was overseas. There were responsibilities that she would have as a service wife that would be different. There would be circumstances she would find herself in as she became part of a biracial couple. Ron would share those responsibilities and circumstances. She would have God and she would have Ron, in that order. Add her parents and her friends into the mix, and she bowed her head and gave thanks to the God that looked after everyone for all the blessings he had bestowed upon her in her short life.

The rest of the day was spent with Sylvia and Ron teaching his parents how to play euchre. Ron had learned when Jenny, Brad, and Sylvia had come to Washington, DC several years ago. He enjoyed the card game, but it appeared that it was a game that only Hoosiers were in love with. He had never heard of it before his friendship with them. His parents enjoyed it once they caught on and the afternoon was spent just getting to know each other.

Sylvia went into the room across from Ron's. She knew that his parents were aware that they had spend nights together, but she was not going to disrespect them enough to go to Ron's room even though it had seemed like such a long time since his arms had held her. She was just about to drift off when she felt the bed dip as Ron crawled in behind her and snuggled close. He had slept in his own room the night before, and she had thought he would again this evening.

He whispered into her ear as he spooned her, "Tomorrow is when we find out how soon we can marry." He kissed her shoulder and rubbed her midriff easing his hand up toward her breasts after taking his hand from her hip to mid thigh as she laid on her side.

She rolled away from him and propped her elbows as she stayed on her stomach and they began to talk. His hands rubbed her ass over and over as they discussed how they hoped the next day went.

"Do you think we can get married tomorrow?"

"Well," Ron said, "we will find out when we get there." He knew that he would never love anyone any more than he could love Sylvia. She was his now and forevermore. He kissed her forehead, then found her lips and pulled her over with him. "Sleep, Baby, sleep," he said as they both drifted off to sleep.

========================

Sylvia woke alone. Ron had awakened early and left her bed so that there would not be any embarrassment on her part when his mom came to wake her up. He had showered early and was downstairs having a cup of coffee with his dad when she came down dressed for the day.

She leaned down and gave him a kiss on the cheek. "I think we can do better than that," he said standing and pulling her toward him with a kiss that was just right but no so intimate as to get her juices flowing or to get him hard. "Good morning."

She blushed and gave a shy smile, since she felt his dad's eyes on her as she stepped away from Ron. "Good morning. That is a lovely way to start my day." She pulled herself toward his lips for another quick peck before she went over to the counter and poured herself a cup of coffee.

Sylvia got up to help Amelia with the dishes and was quickly shooed away. "You kids said you wanted to go to Annapolis today. Just go on and get on the road before traffic gets any more hectic than it will need to be."

Ron and Sylvia arrived at Annapolis about 10:00 am and headed to the Naval Academy Chapel. They had the results of their blood tests and today was the third day of the waiting period. They knew that there would be a conference with the chaplain, and Ron hoped that he would agree to go ahead and marry them that day. He would have until the following Monday before he had to report to the Naval base in Norfolk for his next assignment. Sylvia had requested two weeks off, but had only been granted one week, so they would both travel back to Indiana together, then he would fly back to Norfolk that Monday so they would have as much time together as they could.

They had a deep detailed and open discussion with the chaplain regarding the kinds of stumbling blocks they would be up against. Indiana was historically a Klan state, and, as a result, there could be repercussions when their marriage became known. Ron and Sylvia explained why they wanted to marry at Annapolis and why they were not going to make their marriage common knowledge in Indiana at this time. The chaplain was not sure this was the wisest move on their part, but they had thought it out and he could find no overriding reason not to go ahead and marry them right then.

Sylvia and Ron had checked into a motel in town and were eating at one of the several seafood and crab restaurants available in Annapolis that afternoon for their wedding meal. Ron ordered a good bottle of wine since they were in walking distance of the restaurant. They had a toast to their new life and walked hand in hand to the motel when they were finished. They were unaware of the stares from across the street as Ron unlocked the door to room 103 at the motel.

Trouble Arrives

The dark-haired man flicked his cigarette down and took a swig of the beer he was drinking as he stood outside the bar. He went into the bar to talk to a couple of his friends, telling them about the pretty white girl that was taken into the motel across the street by a nigger. He went on to tell them that he thought that it was about time niggers in this town knew their place. Next thing they knew, the niggers would be grabbing all their girlfriends and wives away from them. Most of the guys realized he was drunk, but the others had been drinking for a while also and began agreeing with him. They decided to go over and have a talk with that nigger.

The bartender picked up the phone and called the police as soon as the men left the bar. That was not the kind of publicity and trouble the small town of Annapolis needed right now.

Ron heard the pounding on the door as Sylvia went into the bathroom. "Lock your door, Baby," he said as he walked toward the outer door. He recognized that the intensity of the knock was not that of housekeeping bringing them extra towels. This was the kind of knock that meant trouble. He heard her click the lock to the bathroom before he opened the door. He had looked out the keyhole and had seen white men standing out there, beers in their hands and cigarettes dangling from their mouths. They were a bit unsteady, so he thought he knew what he might be dealing with. He engaged the chain on the door before opening it.

"How can I help you fellows?" he questioned as he opened the door a crack.

"You can get your ugly black ass out here a minute and let us talk to you right now, Nigger," a dark-haired man slurred.

"No, no, I don't see any need to do that. You already know I am black and I am ugly. I am not sure we have much more to discuss." Ron heard a siren in the background and it sounded like it was nearing, so he felt he only needed to hold these guys at bay and avoid any contact.

"Hey, there, buddy," one of the other guys began, "Darryl here didn't mean to be so nasty, we just wanted to talk to you. You know, get to know you better since you are here in our town."

"Well," Ron continued, "I am only passing through. I am going to Norfolk for my orders overseas. I graduated from the academy a few years ago, and I am just here to visit some old teachers for a day. I will be heading out of town tomorrow. I don't think any of us need any trouble."

"Well now, we do have something to talk about," the guy identified as Darryl continued. "You have a pretty little white girl in there with you. I saw you from across the street. We just want to make sure she knows what she's getting into coming to a motel with an ugly black nigger. She has to be some kind of slut to do that."

Ron knew he was being baited but that set him off in a way that nothing else could have. He would never let Sylvia be the butt of such talk as long as he lived, simply because she had chosen to love him. He closed the door, took the chain off, and stepped out onto the sidewalk.

"You want to repeat that?" he questioned. He stood about three inches taller than the tallest guy and about twenty pounds of pure muscle over the heaviest guy. None of them appeared to have worked out ever, but they were buoyed up by alcohol. And there were three of them.

"I said," he began as the police car pulled into the parking lot and came up to that parking space.

The policeman got out of the car and came over to the men. "Darryl, Sam called me when you guys left the bar. Do we need to go downtown and cool off?"

"Nope," Darryl said as he took a swing at the policeman. He was quickly subdued, cuffed, and put in the police car.

'Now, who is going to be next?" the policeman asked, looking at the other two. Both men put their hands up, looked over at Ron saying, "Sorry, man. We let things get out of hand," and they continued to back off.

"I would suggest you guys get home and sleep it off. I am calling you both cabs. Don't want to be called later and find out you have killed someone by drinking and driving. Ya hear?"

"Yeah, man, we hear ya," one of the men shouted over his shoulder.

The policeman stepped over to Ron before he left with Darryl. "Are you okay?"

"Yeah, but thanks for showing up when you did. It could have been nasty."

The policeman left, and Ron went back into the room. Sylvia had finished her shower and had a towel wrapped around her as she rushed over to step into Ron's open arms. "What was that all about?"

"That was what happens with you cross an ignoramus with a few beers. Don't worry about it, let's get this honeymoon started."

"I am okay with that, Spanky."

"Spanky?"

"Yes, Spanky. I liked the way you were rubbing my ass and I just wondered what it would be like to be spanked. I have read about that, you know, and now that we are married, I wondered if you knew anything about it?"

"Not personally, not really, but I think we could probably figure it out together, and I am sure there are people we could ask," he chuckled.

"Really?"

He laughed a hearty laugh, "No, not really, I don't know anyone, but I have been around guys talking about it and I must admit, the idea of doing that with you has gotten me hard when they have discussed the topic. But you have to remember, I have not been with anyone but you since we met. You weren't my first, but you were close. I am glad now that any expertise I get will be with your beautiful body. We will get there together, and anything you want to try we will try. If I suggest something, and you want to try it, we will. If you don't, we won't. This marriage is going to be full of fun, laughter, and love. Okay?"

"That is quite okay with me," she said as they embraced and began their evening.

The next morning, they woke up late, showered, and had a late breakfast before Ron gave Sylvia her wedding present.

"Oh, Ron, they are beautiful," she said as she opened the box that contained diamond studs for the ears she had pierced a few months ago. "Let me put them in right now."

Ron was lying on his back with his hands behind his head as a truck came crashing into the door of the motel. Sylvia screamed and Ron jumped up, pushed her into the bathroom, and looked around for something to use as a weapon if needed. There was an ironing board and he grabbed the iron.

In through the door came Darryl. "You son of a bitch. I spent the night in jail because of you, you motherfucker! The old lady didn't come bail me out, and when I got home, she had taken the kids and left. It's all your fault, you black son of a bitch."

Ron had never known fear, but even in dangerous situations in Southeast Asia, he had known his enemy. He had known where the enemy was coming from politically, nationally, and what his fighting ability and training was. He could formulate the danger. This guy was an unknown factor, and there was Sylvia to consider. He edged himself toward the phone. It was late enough in the morning that someone would be at the desk. All he had to do was get the receiver off and push zero. If the clerk was attentive, he would already be aware of this altercation and the police would be on their way to the motel.

"Look, buddy, I am sorry about your wife. This isn't going to make the situation any better. Why don't you just calm down and leave." Ron saw that he was armed with a one-inch iron pipe about two-and-a-half feet long. It would be a weapon Ron could easily disarm when the time came.

Darryl lunged at Ron with the pipe overhead. As it came down, Ron dropped the iron, grabbed the pipe, twisted it out of his grip, and threw it behind him as he swung his fist into a clearly landed upper cut followed by a right cross and reached in to put a pressure hold on his shoulder. Darryl dropped and Ron stepped toward him, continuing the pressure hold.

"Sylvia," he called. "Open the door, Baby, it's okay."

She peeked out the bathroom door, fear on her face. Her voice trembled as she asked him, "Are you okay, Ron?"

"I need you to get out of here, go to the front desk, and make sure the police are on their way."

As she left the room through the broken window next to the door that was blocked by Darryl's truck, Ron looked up and realized the police must be on their way since a crowd had gathered outside the room.

As two squad cars arrived, there was also a tow truck entering the parking lot. Ron and Sylvia answered questions. Sylvia was surprised to hear that Ron was surprising her with a four day honeymoon trip to nearby Ocean City, Maryland and had reserved the honeymoon suite at one of the nicer hotels along the Boardwalk.

It was about 2:00 in the afternoon before all the statements were taken and forms filled out. As they checked out, they were not charged for the room, and they quickly got in the car and drove to Ocean City to begin yet another new experience together.

Luckily there was enough of a drive that they were both able to decompress and relax, getting over the bigotry that had been shown by the actions of a small-minded man in Annapolis.

Ocean City, Maryland

The week after Thanksgiving found Ocean City, Maryland abandoned. The quaint town that rose to tens of thousands in the summer was called home by about six thousand people in the winter. This was fine for the honeymooning couple. Ron had made reservations at the Hospitality Inn, in a large room with an enormous bed and a balcony that overlooked the Atlantic Ocean. The hotel was open year around, one of the few that was, and even boasted twenty-four hour room service.

Ron and Sylvia arrived in time to have their evening meal in the dining room after changing clothes once they had arrived. Normally, the two would have been wrapped in each other's arms but the events of the morning had given them pause. It was a conversation they needed to have, but both were dreading.

"Is your steak fixed to your liking, ma'am?" the waiter asked as Sylvia fiddled with her meal, eating very little of the steak as the waiter filled her coffee cup.

"Oh, yes," she said absentmindedly. "It is grilled perfectly, thank you. I just guess I am not as hungry as I thought I was," she continued as she looked up at him with a smile.

Ron looked over at his lovely bride, but he did not know what to say. They had talked little on the way from Annapolis. "Hey, Sweetie. Let's get our coats on and take a walk." His heart ached as she looked up at him with her eyes moistened by tears as she gave him a slight smile and a nod.

They left to grab their coats and scarves the headed to the boardwalk where they had the place all to themselves. While they could hear the waves, it was too dark to see the ocean. It was calming and peaceful yet mysterious. "You know, our marriage is kind of like that ocean."

"Oh, how is that?" she asked at his grip tightened on her hand.

"Well, right now, we can't see much of anything. We know that it is there, but it is hidden. While we can't see the beauty, we can feel the beauty because we hear the waves coming upon the shore. We know it is beautiful because we have had glimpses of it. We also know that the ocean can be treacherous because we have been warned of that. Now the way I look at the ocean is like this. We can focus on the dangers or the beauty. If we look for the danger, we will find it. If we look for the beauty, that is what we will find."

Sylvia stopped and turned toward him putting her arms around his waist as he enfolded her in his big arms. "I get what you are saying, Ron. I get it, and I agree with it. But I have to tell you, I was scared this morning."

"Me too, Sylvia. But there were several issues there. It seemed to be about race, and in his case, it probably was. There had been drinking involved, there had been jail, there had been his wife leaving him, and I am sure that was not the first time that happened. He was a violent unpredictable man at best. The fact that he saw a black man with a white woman fueled that violence. It is not how most people are going to react to us. For every one person like that, there are fifty more who don't care that we are together, or if they do care, they will just leave us alone. They won't drive a fucking truck into a motel room."

Sylvia began giggling, and before long the two were laughing at how ridiculous the entire morning had been. The world was still spinning, and they were married and looking forward to the rest of their lives. They stood hugging each other, letting themselves just soak in the peaceful sound of the ocean waves and allowing it to carry their concerns away.

=========================
====

Thursday morning, Ron rolled over and Sylvia wasn't there. He listened to see if she was moving around in the bathroom and heard nothing. He got out of bed to investigate and looked for a note to see where she had gone. With no note, he decided she had probably gone to get some coffee and rolls to bring back to the room for breakfast. He went ahead and got up, took his shower and got dressed. He opened the door and reached down to get the paper. As the elevator door opened, Sylvia stepped out. She had a large bag full of wood slung over one arm, a bag of food tucked under her elbow, and and two cups of coffee juggled in her hands.

Ron rushed to help relieve her of the coffee and food while she adjusted the big bag. "What on earth do you have there?" he asked.

"Driftwood," she said as though carrying a bag full of pieces of wood into a posh hotel at eight in the morning was an everyday occurrence. "Driftwood and seaglass."

They walked back to the room, and Ron pushed the door open for her to enter.

"It is a collection of the most beautiful pieces of driftwood I could find. I have seen pieces on every walk we have taken, but I just had not picked it up. I realized that it will soon be time for us to be leaving here, and I wanted some to always remind me of our honeymoon. And wait until you see what else I found."

Sylvia was excited as she began taking out unique pieces of wood that had been smoothed by the ocean then gently tossed on the beach. As she brought them out, she shared some of the ideas she had for how she could use them to decorate their home once they were able to have their own place together.

"And now, for your special wedding gift," she smiled reaching in and closing her hand around something. She held it in her fist and told Ron to closed his eyes and held out his hand. She placed something cool in his hand as she told him, "It isn't alive, so don't drop it."

His first instinct was just that, to drop it. It was cool and damp but he held onto it and began working it around in between his fingers. He knew it was a find from the ocean because she had been gathering treasures and it was very smooth. It was a shape he could not quite figure out, rather circular but not quite.

"Can you guess what it is?"

"No, I can't. It is smooth and round. Now, let me see, I can think of something I know that I love that is smooth and round, but it is more than a handful."

Sylvia laughed and smacked his arm. "You are always thinking about some kind of sex."

"No," he said, dropping his voice. "I am always thinking about you and sex just enters my mind from there." He leaned over in the general area of her voice and she met his lips with hers.

"Well, then, open your eyes." She stood back and had a hopeful look on her face as Ron looked at her before seeing what she had given him. He then looked down and saw the most beautiful green colored stone in the shape of a heart. It was small and almost perfectly shaped. "I still have the heart-shaped rock you gave me when we first met. I carry it in my purse and take it out whenever I need to. Whenever I feel lonely, sad, even angry, it soothes me. I hope this can do the same for you."

Ron fought tears as he realize what a gift he had been given with the depth of her love for him. It was a love that people seldom found, and when they did, they often tossed it aside when things got tough. He vowed he would never let that happen to his love for her, and he only hoped he could remain worthy of her love for him.

The two spent the rest of the morning in bed and continued to consummate their union. The next day would be their last day, and Ron had yet another surprise for her. Friday was a bright crisp day, and they had wanted to see some of the other areas of the town. Sylvia couldn't help but laugh as Ron tucked his tall frame into the Corvair. When the time came, they would definitely need a larger car.

"What?" he asked as he saw her stifle a giggle.

"Nothing, I just see you get in this car and think about the clowns getting out of those volkswagens at the Shrine Circus." They both got a laugh out of that picture as they headed out of the parking lot and onto the main thoroughfare. "Where are we going?"

"I was here years ago with my grandparents when I stayed with them one summer. They brought a couple of my cousins and me up here for part of the vacation time we had with them. I loved it and thought maybe some day I might live here. When I am out of the service, or before, would you ever consider buying a house and living here?"

Sylvia didn't have to take long to consider her answer. "I love it here; of course I would consider it. We don't have to decide today, do we?"

"No," he laughed. "I think we have a few years, but I just wanted to look around some of the areas in town if you were agreeable."

"Well, Spanky, let's get this show on the road and begin our fantasy," she said with a wink.

"Watch what you say around me when you get that look in your eye," he retorted.

The two looked around different neighborhoods and liked them all. If there was one problem, it was that Ron had seen no other black faces except at the hotel where there were a few black couples. He had not seen any resistance to them as a couple by staff at the hotel, nor did he sense any hostility as they stopped for gas. Maybe this was just a piece of heaven that hadn't been discovered yet.

Life Continues

Since it was the holidays and he had just arrived back in the states, Ron had been assigned temporary duty at the Academy. He was one of the junior officers teaching strategies classes. This worked especially well since he had served a three-year tour of duty already. He could speak from field experience, and he could also address specifics of work in Southeast Asia since it appeared that the war was not going to end as quickly as had once been hoped for. It also hadn't hurt that he had received two commendations for service above and beyond the call of duty.

Ron and Sylvia spoke almost daily, and their conversations were filled with not only endearments but also some of the practicalities of married life, even though they had neither one shared the marriage with their parents. Everyone just accepted that Ron and Sylvia had spent that time learning more about each other. They had decided that after their honeymoon they should at least tell their parents they were engaged. Neither set of parents fully endorsed the amount of time they spent alone, and an announcement would assuage any questions on their part about their intent to make their relationship permanent.

Sylvia felt that her parents could sense a difference, but they never questioned her. She had proven to be trustworthy in every respect and as Linda and Brian talked, it would probably serve them very well if they did not broadcast the engagement. There was no reason to borrow trouble.

Ron and Sylvia both were counting the days until the Christmas break at her school began. She now understood the true meaning when someone said, "a watched pot never boils."

Sylvia flew to Baltimore and Ron was waiting to pick her up after her school break began. This was going to be the first of many Christmases together and they were looking forward to their time after spending the last three weeks apart. They knew there would be more time spent apart, so they already treasured those times together.

Ron's folks joined them for a couple of days after Christmas then returned home. The two lovers spent most of their time in Ron's apartment enjoying each other. The day after his parents left, the two were watching television when there was a knock on the door. They looked at each other, not knowing who would have been coming to visit on a Sunday afternoon.

Ron got up off the couch and grabbed the bat he kept by the door. "Yes?" he said through the door. "Who is it?"

"Jane Fonda," came the muffled reply.

Ron roared as he swung open the door and greeted Brad. Sylvia jumped up and ran over to get in on all the hugging too. "Brad!! Why didn't you let us know you were coming?"

"Well, Sweetie," he said as her hugged her and swung her around. "I didn't know until they loaded me up and said I had a break for a few days. Stuff is heating up," he said as he gave a worried look to Ron while still hugging Sylvia, "and I don't expect to even be home long enough to visit Mom and Dad. Since I knew from your letters where you would be, I decided you guys are stuck with me for the holidays."

"Oh, Brad. We are so glad you are here. We have so much to catch up on. Can I get you something to eat? A drink?" Sylvia rushed.

"Hold on, Sweet Cheeks," Brad laughed. I need to get to a motel and get situated first.

"You will no such thing," said Ron. "We have the room here and insist you stay."

"Yes, please do, Brad," Sylvia pleaded, not hardly waiting for Ron to get his invitation out.

He looked over at Ron, "If you are sure." Ron nodded and Brad went back out in the hall and grabbed his duffel and put it on the flowered chair that sat in the corner.

"Now, can I fix you a sandwich? or I have some leftover lasagna," Sylvia said with a grin, knowing Brad loved her lasagna.

"Sylvia, that is about the best Christmas gift I can imagine. I would love some lasagna."

The friends stayed up until after midnight talking over old times and new. Brad had made friends with one of the nurses in the field hospital in South Vietnam. He insisted it wasn't serious, but Sylvia wasn't so sure. According to Brad, they had agreed to rub each other's itch for the time they were together. He did seem to regret that he had not had a chance to say goodbye to her, but he had plans on sending her a silver bracelet as a late Christmas gift to let her know he would always value their time together.

The next morning, Brad took a bus to Washington, DC and reported to the Pentagon. He had been given a field promotion for his undercover work and awaited his next deployment. He found that he would be given a week off. He made plane reservations, took the bus back to Annapolis, picked up his bag from Ron and Sylvia's, said his goodbyes, and headed to Indiana to visit with his parents. They all made plans to meet up in DC the day before he was due to fly out the next week.

Ron crawled into bed that night as Sylvia was turned on her side away from him. He pushed her onto her stomach and began giving her a backrub after putting lotion on his hands and warming it before he touched her back. The rub continued as he gave most of his attention to her nicely rounded cheeks. "You are a warm, sexy woman. My warm, sexy woman. You light me up like a rocket. I can spend hours with you, enjoying your body. Is it any different for a woman?"

"I am not sure I can answer that," Sylvia replied. "I could lay here all night feeling you rub my back and my butt. It feels so good knowing that we are heading into a new part of our lives." The couple laid there for a few hours simply exploring each other's bodies as two newlyweds are apt to do.

============================
====

Ron and Sylvia woke up late and, after the acrobatics and exercise of the night before, had a leisurely day waiting for the classes at the Academy to resume. Sylvia had to leave on New Year's Day since her classes took back up on January 2.

Ron had received word before break that unless something changed he would be finishing the semester and would probably be called upon to take over classes for other officers who were due to move to other positions. He and Sylvia had looked at the calendar and had discussed the different ways they could get back and forth during the time she would be in school. If their luck lasted, they would be spending the summer together again.

Luck didn't last. Sylvia received a call from Ron in January. General Leonard Chapman had replaced General Wallace Greene as commandant of the Marines. Because of the close connection between the Navy and the Marines, Ron had once again been requisitioned, as an asset, to accompany the General to Saigon. He was to receive a promotion and special dispensation in order to serve as chief strategy advisor to the General. It was a significant promotion, and could not Ron have refused it even if he wanted to. This position would keep him on the fast track in his career, and then as soon as the war was over, he would have more of a chance at getting the assignment of his choice stateside. The call to Sylvia was not an easy one to make, but he requested a three-day weekend so he could fly up on a Friday and be at her house when she got out of school.

When Sylvia entered the back door that afternoon she heard voices in the living room and one sounded like Ron. It couldn't be ,but she went in to see who was visiting. Her heart jumped as he stood and turned and she ran into his arms. "Ron. Oh, Ron. I have missed you so much. I love you."

It didn't matter to her that her parents were both sitting there. They knew the couple was in love, planning on marriage as soon as they could, and were both looking toward the day when Ron would be done with the war.

"I have a three day weekend. Things have been shaking in Southeast Asia. The Marines have had a major change in command, and I have been promoted to an adjunct position in Saigon. I leave on Monday and will probably be gone two years." He paused for breath. "I don't know any other way to say it. I have rented a car and intend to take you to Indy for a couple of days before I have to get back and deploy."

=========================

The respite was over almost as soon as it began. Sylvia had never been as sad as she was when she said goodbye to Ron that Sunday afternoon. She knew this would be their life for many years. She just had not realized it would hurt so badly.

Two Years of Hell

Worries in Indiana

Sylvia was having a difficult time keeping her mind on her teaching. She had very supportive friends at school and her parents were great. She had planned to fly down to Richmond and spend her spring break with Ron's parents in mid-April of 1968. She hoped it would make her feel closer to them.

Ron had written faithfully for the first couple of months, then he advised her that things were getting rough and he might not be able to write as often and for her not to worry. The news in mid-March was some of the worst of the war. Men in the Charlie Company had been involved in a massive battle in My Lai, a village in Vietnam. There were not a lot of details, and though other battles were happening, journalists kept coming back to this story because of the horrific losses. The American troops were getting frustrated. The jungle terrain was not an easy one to conquer, and as American losses mounted and the protests about U.S. involvement reached the soldiers, morale was low.

On April 4, 1968, the world took another spin, and Sylvia felt the ripples. Dr. Martin Luther King, Jr. was assassinated in Tennessee. The world was in mourning, at least the black world was, and with it were those closely aligned with the black population whether by birth, marriage, friendship, or by devotion to the cause of equality.

Being with the Michaels helped all of them heal and helped them deal with the absence of Ron. They filled their time with philosophical and social discussions and enthusiastic games of rummy. Amelia helped Sylvia learn how to cook some of Ron's favorite foods. She got to see the photo albums and scrapbooks of Ron as a small boy growing up. She asked pointed questions about some of the issues she did not understand concerning perceived differences between the white and black cultures. Differences that had nothing to do with skin color but rather cultural traditions.

Time Drags

The days dragged and Sylvia used the summer to finish work on her Master's degree in Education. The state required that a teacher start on it within five years of getting their Bachelor's then finish it within five years of starting it. The teacher would then possess a lifetime teaching license. The three years Ron had been in Southeast Asia, she had taken summer classes so she wouldn't need to add evening classes to her work load during the year. She was only two classes away from her advanced degree, and both classes she wanted to take were available so she went ahead and finished that degree. She also checked into adding a couple of endorsement classes that would enable her to teach middle school children. It would give her more marketability when she was able to join Ron later in their marriage.

Peace talks had begun in Paris in the spring, and Sylvia found herself listening to the news every day hoping to hear of movement in that direction. Then in June the Marines began to withdraw from Khe Sanh. Sylvia had hoped to hear that Ron would be coming home, but his letters indicated that he was as safe as he could be, but his position as strategic advisor would not be a short assignment.

The world shattered and rocked again in early June when Robert Kennedy, brother to the assassinated president Kennedy, was assassinated in the kitchen of a hotel while he was campaigning for the Democratic Presidential nomination. There were anti-war riots in Chicago at the 1968 Democratic National Convention. Sylvia was beginning to wonder if the world would ever become right again.

The lazy hazy draggy days of summer finally gave way to the crisp days of autumn. The Greenes invited James and Amelia up for the Thanksgiving holiday and promised they would come down for Christmas that winter of 1968. The families were beginning to blend as they all recognized that their families were truly intertwined. Sylvia had written to Ron and told him that she would like to set a date for their "wedding" and hoped it would be over Christmas in 1970, or as near that as possible. Ron thought that sounded like a good plan because he was reasonably sure that his deployment would be over by that time.

Sylvia announced those plans to both sets of parents and the Carvers on Thanksgiving. She was surprised when Brad's parents brought Helen Bradley with them for dinner. Brad and Helen had dated for two years in high school but had parted after graduation. It appeared that when he had been home over Christmas they had revived their relationship, and the Carvers confided to Linda that they were expecting Brad to propose the next time he was home. Sylvia was surprised to hear this. She wrote Brad regularly, and he had mentioned nothing about this. It would be interesting to hear what he had to say when he did finally tell her.

Ron did manage to get a call through to his parents and Sylvia on Christmas day. She loved being able to talk to him, but after he hung up, she just missed him that much more. She had to learn to deal with this. He would not be giving up the life he had planned and studied for. He had served four years already and would be in at least sixteen years more, and as they had talked, it was really more like serving for about forty years altogether.

She was lucky that she had such supportive family members or she wasn't sure how she would make it through. The year 1969 began with Richard Nixon's inauguration as he named Henry Kissinger as his Secretary of State. Everyone thought that would be a good placement because he seemed to be a good negotiator. Peace talks had broken down barely before they had started, and when Ho Chi Minh died in September people waited to see what would happen. In November of 1969 it was revealed what had really happened in My Lai. The frustrated troops had gone in the small village with a "search and destroy" order and had methodically massacred over three hundred unarmed civilians, including children. It was a time of even more protests over the war.

It was the second Christmas that Sylvia would be without Ron and she had learned to work and live a solitary life. One in which she was married, yet did not have the comfort of being able to share that with her friends and family. It would be a relief to her when she could at least begin planning the wedding they would have with their friends. It would be a renewal of vows for them, a public affirmation of their love and commitment.

This year the families flipped and spent Thanksgiving in Virginia and would be spending Christmas in Indiana. The days passed quickly. Sylvia had transferred from a fifth grade classroom at the lab school to a sixth grade departmentalized public school in Bloomington. She was teaching science and enjoying it very much. It gave her a new focus, and she had spent much of her time this year setting about working on new lesson plans, which had helped her deal with Ron's deployment.

Happy New Year

On the morning of December 31st, New Year's Eve, Sylvia had just finished cleaning the upstairs bathroom and had headed into her bedroom to dust when her mother called her down to help get something out of a tall cabinet. When she said she would be there in a few minutes, she heard someone coming up the stairs and as she turned around, Ron's arms went around her and they both collapsed onto the bed after Ron kicked the door shut on his way in.

"Oh, God!" Sylvia clutched at Ron as they held each other as closely and as tightly as it was humanly possible. Ron had shed his coat in the kitchen before coming upstairs but they quickly divested each other of their clothes and began an exploration that ended as Ron pressed into Sylvia's wet core with movements that began so rapid and hard then melted into slow and sensual then quickly heated up again so that they both came with an intensity that made it impossible to be quiet.

Sylvia gave a soft giggle. "I can't believe we were that loud with my parents downstairs. What will they be thinking?"

"Honey, baby, they don't think, they know. They were young once, and I hope they are still young enough to enjoy each other like this."

At that remark, Sylvia laughed. "I hope they do to, but somehow, I don't think they pound into each other quite the same way we do."

Both chuckled as they laid in each other's arms. The sensuous feelings began to build again, and this time Ron entered her taking her to heaven and back before he came.

Sylvia was laying on her back when she suddenly propped upon her elbows, "Ron. Do you realize we forgot a condom? Both times."

"Oh, damn, Baby. It didn't even enter my mind. I had such a need for you. Is this a bad time for that to happen?"

Sylvia thought a minute and shook her head, "No, I don't think so."

Ron relaxed. The idea of a baby with Sylvia made him happy. They had discussed wanting two or three children. They had both come from single child families and agreed that they wanted children to have brothers and sisters to fight with. He had moved heaven and earth to get this break and knew he would be going back in a few days. He hoped he could talk Sylvia into going ahead and getting married in the church on short notice. His parents could be there on a twenty-four hour notice so he rolled toward her and began his quest.

"Sylvia, let's not wait to get married. Let's do it this weekend."

"Okay."

"I think my parents can get up here and we.... What? Did you say 'okay'?"

"Yes, you crazy man, yes, yes, yes. I will run away with you today and get married. But, there is one thing to say."

"What's that?" he asked.

"You do remember we are already married, don't you?"

Ron laughed. "You know, sometimes I almost forget. Maybe we just need to get my parents up here and let them all know at the same time."

"I think that sounds perfect. Call your parents then go to the store with me. We can get the fixings for my lasagna, and we can even cut a piece and set a place for Brad and pretend he is here to enjoy it with us. If it hadn't been for Brad, we would never have met."

"Now, there, I have to disagree, Love. We would have met somewhere, sometime. I don't know how, but our paths have crossed in other lifetimes. We are here, now, together, because our lives could be no other way."

Sylvia nestled into his arms and relaxed into his embrace, knowing that their love was very special.

Surprise, Surprise

Ron and Sylvia got back from the grocery store. Ron began cutting the vegetables for the salad while Sylvia began layering the lasagna. Ron had put a tape in the deck of favorite songs that he had a friend copy for him.

Ron's parents arrived and the Carvers were invited over to join them for supper. The conversation centered around the war, its developments, and Brad. His parents had received a letter just that day and shared it with them.

Hey, Mom, Dad --

Love you guys! I have been working on learning to whittle. I know, it sounds crazy. There is an old man here in the village who whittles these beautiful buddhas from the wood that is native here. It is some kind of teak, which will last forever. To carve it, you have to know which branches to cut. He showed me how to test them. The hard branches are the ones used for furniture, but sometimes there are sucker branches that can be carved. It is a little bit like the sucker branches on tomatoes, ya know?

I must admit, my figures don't look like his but there are 2 or 3 that I will keep. I give my discards to the kids on the village along with a candy bar. I am sure they pitch the figurine, but they do love the candy bars so at least they wait until I am not in sight before they ditch the wood. Hahahah.

I guess you have heard that they are beginning to scale back any more deployments. I think I may be close to getting out of here. I can't say a whole lot about the place I am now. It is secure classified and so is the job I am doing. I can tell you, I think, unless it gets blacked out, that it is a relatively safe job. If I can stay here for the next few months, I will have enough carved figurines for all the people on my Christmas list for the next five years… or we can have a big bonfire when I get home. I miss Indiana. Never thought I would say, that, but I really do. We just didn't realize how lucky we were growing up until you get out of your little spot in the world and see what goes on elsewhere.

Ron is home, and he said he would be seeing you guys before he came back. He is one helluva great guy. I know he and Sylvia are crazy about each other. They have some stormy weather ahead of them, but I only hope I can find someone to care about like he cares about her. Lucky man. Give him my best if you see him…

Even though we are still under the same command over here, it has been three months since I have been in the same village. It is just crazy, but hopefully it will be over soon. Next Christmas I plan on being home.

Happy New Year.

Gotta go folks. Will write back when I can. Hope to hear from you soon. Love you both.   Brad

"Oh," said Sylvia, as the tears welled up in her eyes. "I hate to think of Brad over there alone while we are all here."

"He knows we always hold him in our hearts, dear," said Mrs. Carver. "He knows that. And, he knows that you and Ron are right there with him too at this time of year, and always."

The group was sombre as they ate their meal. After the dessert had been served and the coffee poured, Ron stood up and they all looked up at him. "Sylvia and I have something we need to share with you," he began.

Brian and Linda looked at each other, figuring what was coming.

"Sylvia and I got married when I was injured. We married at Annapolis and before you get really upset with us, I want to explain. We know," and he nodded to include his parents in the term "we," "that when a black person falls in love with a white person, it can create problems for the families, both of them. Right now, it is not popular for the races to do what they are calling 'mixing.'"

Ron looked down at Sylvia. Then he looked over at the Greenes. "I love your daughter more than life itself and I will lay down my life to protect her. The country will not always be like this, but now it is, and that was why we kept this a secret for so long."

"Ron," Brian said as he reached over and grabbed Linda's hand, "we appreciate your concern and you know that we share that concern, I cannot deny that. We know your love is not the question, and we will support you in any way we can. We are concerned about Sylvia's safety but we know that you love each other. People won't understand the kind of love that crosses boundaries that have been set up."

Linda stood up and went over to hug them both. "You just need to remember what you loved about each other when you fell in love every time you ask yourself, 'What in the world was I thinking?'" She and Brian looked at each other and laughed, then were joined by the Carvers and the Michaels.

James spoke up, "Yes, son, Brian is right... that will happen, count on it."

Ron looked over at Sylvia and gave a shrug then began again, "I got some champagne this afternoon and thought we could have a toast."

The group enjoyed the rest of the evening with the older couples sharing funny tales with the "newlyweds."

The Carvers were the first to decide that it was time they got back home, followed by Ron's parents.

Before they left for the motel that Ron had reserved for them, he felt that he needed to make an additional apology to the Greenes. "I hope you will forgive us, but the racial issue is one that will become more pronounced now that others know we are married. I am sure many people think that we are simply friends. They find that curious enough. When they find out we love each other and have pledged our lives together, it may make enemies of those we have thought were friends. We wanted to postpone that as long as we possibly could, for all our sakes. Whatever lies ahead of us, people will not understand that we all see each other equally with love as in any other family. They see differences. We see each other's soul, not their skin. For this, I am very hopeful for all of us. On another front, Sylvia and I neither enjoyed keeping this a secret. It allowed you to make assumptions about the commitment we felt and the intimacy involved. Sylvia and I would not have taken that last step if we had not been committed and for us that meant to go ahead and get married."

Brian reached his hand out to shake Ron's. "I know that son."

Linda was hugging Sylvia as there were tears in her eyes. "You take care of yourself and we will be talking," she told her daughter.

Wedding Night Banter

Ron unlocked the door and opened it. Sylvia stepped into a fairyland. There were Christmas tree lights wound into garland and strewn around the credenza. A silver ice bucket held champagne, and sitting next to it was a dish of chocolate covered strawberries. Sylvia smiled as she looked up at him. "This is beautiful." She put her arms around his waist as he pulled her close to him. "Thank you for making our lives so special."

"I hope you feel that way when I am gone for months at a time on deployment through the years."

"I miss you when you are out of my sight. You know I will miss you like this, but my darling, you are always with me."

The two stood for a moment, just holding each other. Ron reached over and turned on the cassette recorder. "May I?" he asked as he began dancing with her to "Our Day Will Come."

"Did we ever think that we would actually get here to this point in time?"

"I knew we would from the first time we danced to this song, honey."

Sylvia sighed and knew that whatever happened, this would be one of the best days in her life.

EPILOGUE

Nine Months Later

"AAAHHHHHH!" Sylvia screamed. "I do not know that I am ever going to let Ron forget this."

"Now, Sylvia, calm down. Breathe. In. Out. In. Out. That's it," Shelly said.

"Where is he? He is halfway across the damned world, that's where!! He needs to be here. He needs to be here with me." Sylvia felt another pain take over her and began to panic.

"Breathe, Sylvia. In. Out. In. Out."

"Shelly, if you weren't a nurse, I would pop you one good," she retorted as she tried to follow directions. She looked up at all of the metal hanging down over her as Shelly said, "Okay, I see the head. Beautiful black haired baby there, Sylvia. One last push. Come on. One big push. That's it! You did it! It is a beautiful little boy, Sylvia. We didn't need that doctor, we women can birth babies all by ourselves."

Both women laughed at the *Gone With the Wind* reference. Shelly had handed the baby off to be checked by the internist who had just entered the room. When he was finished he brought the baby over to show Sylvia.

"Can I hold him?"

"Not quite yet. We need to let you rest for a few minutes and put him in the nursery. You can see him shortly. Have you thought of a name for him?"

"Brandon Wesley Michaels," she replied.

"Well, Brandon Wesley Michaels, let's get you in that nursery. You are going to be the only boy in there with three little girls. That is a lucky beginning for you." He handed the baby to Shelly for her to take to the nursery.

Before Shelly left, she held the baby close to Sylvia who rubbed his cheek with the back of her fingers very lightly and whispered, "I love you, Brandon."